Rachael Shaw was born and raised in Sheffield. She is the 3rd of 4 daughters and has a west highland terrier named Lola.

Rachael took up writing just as a hobby to help with personal struggles and it soon became her passion. Her stories developed as part of a method to help her sleep at night.

Something Beyond the Pages – a world that is hidden, is her debut novel.

To my parents, sisters and my fluff ball Westie, Lola.

In memory of my nannan, Margaret Rich. Always in our hearts, never forgotten.

Rachael Shaw

Something Beyond the Pages

A World That Is Hidden

Austin Macauley Publishers™
London • Cambridge • New York • Sharjah

A CIP catalogue record for this title is available from the British Library.

ISBN 9781398400627 (Paperback)
ISBN 9781398400634 (ePub e-book)

www.austinmacauley.com

First Published 2021
Austin Macauley Publishers Ltd®
1 Canada Square
Canary Wharf
London
E14 5AA
+44 (0)20 7038 8212
+44 (0)20 3515 0352

Thanks to my mum and my dad, for helping me through the whole process.

My sisters, for being as annoying as ever…in a supportive way.

Bobbie Richardson, for encouraging me to go for it.

Day in, day out, I'd sit and imagine what life would be like if I had the life I dreamed of; if I had the confidence to stand up and say to the world, here I am, I'm coming to take you on! If there were some sort of magic, spells, and potions which I knew about. Maybe a world where I am the centre, I am needed, really, really needed; I wish for that life. One where I am part of something, something that not everyone is part of, something big but not big for everyone.

I can dream but not all dreams can come true. Some are impossible, difficult for people to imagine or even start to believe. Not for me; I believe the impossible may be possible. Some may say I'm in a world of my own.

Chapter One

I agreed, not really knowing why, to go to the bookstore for my mum. She's reading a series of books and finished the third of the series quicker than she expected and somehow, it's my problem. So, now, here I am walking down the street at 5 pm on a Sunday, looking for a bookstore that is open, not that I know where any are. As I'm not a reader, I don't really pay attention to anywhere that sells books, or libraries, for that matter. I can tell you where every clothes' store is in the area and beyond though; I class it as a talent.

To be honest, I am being sent on this errand because my mum just wants me out of the house. Apparently, I have been a typical teenager lately; what even is a typical teenager? She says I am moody, argumentative, always think I know best, dramatic, never out of bed and don't know what a sweeping brush is. I don't agree with those comments but my dad does; how he can comment though, I don't know. I don't think he has looked up from his newspaper since I was born. Something I joke about quite a lot but my parents don't find remotely funny. All I get is, "Cut the attitude, lady, or you can make your jokes at boarding school". Ha! They would never send me to boarding school; it's all empty threats. I just roll my eyes and head back upstairs to lay in my bed and die of boredom. The streets are bare and there are endless closed signs on doors. I haven't come across a bookstore yet; is there one around here even? Am I wasting my time and energy walking around for a shop that may not be open, which will come as no surprise given the time, and I'm quite sure it won't come as a shock to my mother either because she knows full well, one will not be open. She said that I may as well try to look for a shop and when she is done with the book, I can happily read it, which will not be happening on this planet or the next, because as we all know, I do not read! I like to make up my own little stories that include me laying back and imagining myself in different scenarios. Fighting off a dragon to get to the prince, which is a charming twist on a fairy tale, someone depending on me to save the day and I win; I win all the time in my stories.

The heavens have opened, and rain is pouring on my freshly washed hair. I duck for shelter under the canopies sheltering the shops. I haven't brought a coat as rain wasn't on the cards and it's quite warm, being summer and all. So here I am, a walking puddle, my ginger hair is now a tangled mess preparing to be curly and wild when dry. Just my luck, I have stood right under a part of the canopy that happens to have a broken drain showering me with water, typical!

I am just about to give in, head home empty-handed after five minutes of waiting for the rain to settle when I feel something rest on my shoulder. I look slightly to the side to see a hand, wrinkled, signs of old age. My body feels heavy. I'm holding my breath scared to move any more. I can't move anyway, I am frozen to the spot for what has only been a mere few seconds but feels like a lifetime.

“I’m sorry dear, I didn’t mean to scare you,” a sudden calm feeling crosses my body. The voice is soft, aged, matching the hands, “It’s very rainy out there, come in. I was just about to close up. It will give you some time to call someone to pick you up, while staying dry.”

I face the woman, she has a kind smiley face; she’s standing in the doorway of a little shop that looks like it has been here for a long time with very minimal updates. I didn’t hear a door open, but the rain is so heavy it is difficult to hear anything. I decide to go into the shop as I am wondering what the inside is like, and a dry place is very welcome to me at this time.

The inside is dated, like its structure. I stand and take a look around taking it all in; it’s hard not to, as it is quaint. The walls are painted in a dark muddy brown matching the floor. The light shade is a mighty chandelier almost too big for the room and hidden behind a layer of rust, not producing as much light as expected from its grandness, and a few bulbs are out. The lady is shuffling towards the counter, she then starts rattling around behind the desk, before pulling out a dated phone.

“I have a phone you can use; you may need to hold it hard down on to your ear. It’s not the best of phones but it does the job,” I start walking towards her before I realise, I am in a shop that sells books, lots of books, on floor to ceiling bookcases.

“I couldn’t look at your books, could I? I’ve actually been looking for a bookstore, so it’s funny or luck, I guess, that I have stumbled upon here,” I smile hopefully. I’m not sure if the book I am looking for will be here. The books look incredibly old, all brown or black, ancient-looking but it's worth a try.

The lady smiles back, "Of course, you can."

I ponder on where the book may be, if here. I run my finger along them neatly placed books in alphabetical order but never seen a duster, attractive but unknown by me. The lady appears behind me; she's very silent like a ninja.

"You okay, dear, need any help?" Just taking in her attire, I stare at her a short while longer than I should. She's wearing a big cream woolly jumper with little blue beads attached scattered around, a long maroon skirt but not long enough to cover her odd socks, one yellow and one green both stripy, with brown sandals which are too small and very battered.

"Erm, it's okay actually, I don't think you have what I am looking for, but thank you. Am I still okay to use your phone?"

She nods and moseys back towards the counter. I follow, she props herself up on the stool and tucks a strand of her long grey hair that has escaped from her messy bun behind her ear, before pulling the phone towards her with a shaky hand.

"It's very temperamental, got to give it a bit of a knock before using it," she explains before lightly tapping it on the surface. She puts it to her ear, checking for the dial and reaches her arm out, the phone resting in her hand. "Should work now."

I accept the phone and start to dial my house number. It rings a few times before a male voice starts to speak.

"Hello."

"Hi, Dad, it's me. Could you give me a lift home, the rain's awful."

Silence.

"Dad?"

"Who is it?"

"I called you Dad, who else calls you Dad for you to not know who it is. I'm an only child. Did you hear what I said about the rain?"

"What you on about; rain…are you pulling my leg? There's no rain, stop being lazy and walk. Whose phone are you on, anyway?" I can hear Mum in the background asking who he's speaking to.

"It's Adalyn, she wants a lift back." Now I hear her flapping, attempting to get the phone from Dad.

"Is she lost? I only asked her to go to the bookstore, it's ten minutes away. Whose phone she on?"

Dad returns to the phone, "Hello, you still there? Whose phone you on?"

"I'm using a shop phone. That's not the point; what you on about, it's not raining? Have you looked outside," I ask in a confused tone.

"Don't cheek me, it's not raining and you're not getting a lift, goodbye," then, all I can hear is a long dial.

I turn to face the window; the rain has gone. Weird, I could just hear it pouring a matter of minutes ago. Surely, I'm not losing my mind, maybe it's only just stopped. The lady is messing under the counter again; she pulls out a large purple book that almost looks like a work of art. It's like no other book I have seen, it's got raised markings in gold running all over it, but not ruining the look of the beautiful ombre purple that covers the whole of the front and the back.

"Would you be interested in taking this book off my hands?" the lady asks.

"Me?" I reply, longing to know why she would ask.

"I don't actually have enough money on me. My mum would go mad if she knows I bought something with her book money and I know I don't have enough to buy that; it looks very expensive. That's not to say I don't want it but, hmm, I'm sorry, I am sure someone else will want it," I smile, in an apologetic way.

She smiles wide. I notice she has very straight teeth but more on the yellow side, like she smokes a lot. "Don't be silly, you can have it for free, no price."

"I couldn't possibly take it off you for nothing. It is really appealing, but I just think someone else will find it more useful as I am not a keen reader and to give something away that precious for free, just seems obscene."

"It is not to be read, my dear. You will find it more useful than anyone ever could; it just needs a bit of help, a fresh face to bring it back to perfect form. I've had my use out of it," hopefulness fills her eyes; her tone sounds definite, like she really wants me to take it.

"Thank you, I don't know about getting books back to a perfect form, but I could try, I guess. Is it just cleaning it? I have never cleaned a book. Is there some special solution or is it just soap and water?"

"You'll know, when the time comes to fix it. For now, leave it be, make sure it doesn't get into the wrong hands." She's now moving towards the door. She opens the door, still hugging the book, "You must get going, it is extremely late now, your parents will start to worry. It's not just any old book, my sweet, it's special."

She hands me the book and closes the door, with me on the outside before I could reply. She changes the open sign to close, pulls down the blind and then she is gone.

Chapter Two

I open the front door and am greeted with a mouthful by my parents. "Where the hell have you been, what time do you call this,"…blah blah blah. I just head straight upstairs, sit on my bed crossed-legged, and place the book in front of me, ready to see the content. Nothing; there is nothing in the book, just blank page after blank page. All the pages look like when you have a project at school, and you want your paper to look more rustic, so you whip out the tea bags to make that paper look like an ancient scroll that you personally went to find, and dig up, specially to impress.

Am I meant to write in it, like a diary? The lady, whose name I never asked, said I will find it more useful than anyone else, and that she has had her use out of it. There is nothing inside it, what could you possibly do with an empty book except write in it. Unless she wrote in pencil and rubbed it all out, so someone else could have their turn to write in it? Maybe I should do that, or maybe not, it sounds a bit pointless. She could have used invisible ink. I used to have a pen where you wrote with it, then shined a light over it to reveal what you just put; I wonder if I still have it hidden somewhere.

I don't even have anywhere to put the book either, it's quite big. I could put it under my bed, but don't books get wrecked in darkness, or is that in sunlight, or have I just made that up. I probably made that up, but I don't want to risk it so on the top of my wardrobe, it goes.

I must have fell asleep while lost in thought, curiosity doesn't half make you tired. I drag myself up, unaware of my surrounding or time, moving like a zombie, eyes as heavy as weights. I trip over a stray object, not knowing what it is because it could be one of many items that don't have a place and have taken up residence on my floor. "Owwww, owwwiiee, owww." I sit on the edge of my bed to check the damage the anonymous object has caused. No signs of cuts or bruising, but a massive rip has been made in the side of my sock; great. I go downstairs looking for snacks; I make a run for the kitchen before my parents spot me and give me the third degree again. Too late.

"Are you going to tell your dad and me what took you so long and what was that book you had? Did you not get my book I asked for? I'm guessing you forgot and spent my money on a book, you know full well, you won't read." Mum stood, resting on the kitchen counter, eyebrows raised, sipping on a cup of coffee.

I roll my eyes, "No, I didn't get your book and FYI, my book was free and it's not to read." I scatter the money out in front of her, to show her it is all still there. Why do Mum and Dad only ever buy healthy stuff?

"Oh no, you didn't rob it, did you? Is that why you were so long? Oh, Adalyn, I knew you were a trouble causer, but stealing? That's a whole new level," she starts calling out the kitchen door. "Jerry, come here, Adalyn's got herself in some trouble." Huh, what's happening?

"I really didn't expect this from you. Your dad is going to be so ashamed and so am I, rightly so," her arms are now folded, she is shaking her head and I'm stuck in confusion to even realise what is going on.

Next second, Dad comes storming in. "What has she done now, Anne, I told you she is trouble. Jack, from golf, told me about a perfect boarding school that he sends his kids to."

"Wait, what? I never stole anything. The lady at the bookshop gave it to me. I like how you just jumped to your wrong conclusions; I can't believe you thought I'd steal."

They look at each other, speaking through just their eyes, before Mum turns to me and starts to speak again.

"I don't know any more with you. You have been a right mare lately; nothing surprises me anymore."

"I'm not a kid, please don't treat me like one," I shout back.

"Don't answer your mum back. You are just a kid and while you are under this roof, you will show respect."

I storm out slamming my half-bitten apple on the side to show annoyance. How dare they accuse me of stealing and then tell me to show respect, and just a kid! Is he joking? I'm fifteen now, that's basically an adult. I can do what I want, I am verging on womanhood. Ergh, I can't believe them! They are so mean nowadays.

Me and my mum used to be so close when I was younger. We would gossip about everything and everyone, we would giggle over stupid things, we had the same sense of humour and Mum were a big kid at heart. Even my dad used to laugh, which you wouldn't have guessed, as he can't even crack a smile now at things that are actually funny. Things changed; time went by fast, they became busy, I became more independent, we grew apart. Sometimes, when I'm laid in my bed bored, thinking about life, I can't help but remember the good times and shed a tear at the memories.

Back in bed, waiting for the apology that will never come…I sat with my ear to the floor for a while, I heard boarding school crop up a lot. Surely, it's too late now to send me to boarding school, there has to be an age restriction: I'm not going even if they send me, anyway.

I was thinking, I might go back to the bookstore tomorrow, ask a few questions about the book. I just need to remember where about the shop is...

Next day I rise, the sun is shining through the window creating an alluring, happy feeling in my room and making me perk up a bit, even though it is impossible to be happy in a house where you are treated like a stupid child. I throw my clothes on and head downstairs, trying to make as little noise as possible. I swear they sense when I am coming, Dad just happens to be in the hallway, clearly waiting for me to get to the bottom.

"Morning, going anywhere fun?" Well, that was surprisingly polite for someone that accused me of stealing the other day.

"Just out, thought I'd go for a stroll. Want to join?" I reply sarcastically. I carry on walking towards the door, not particularly wanting his reply or waiting for it.

"Oh, right, I was thinking of going for a walk myself actually. I'll take you up on that offer. Your mum is at gardening club."

Oh gosh, what does he want, he is being polite, and he never joins me on a walk; is he going to tell me I'm going to boarding school? I smile back with uncertainty. He pulls his slippers off and swaps them with his outdoor shoes.

We saunter in silence for minutes before he starts to speak, "Delightful day, isn't it?" He's walking with his hands behind his back, looking around like he's never experienced the outdoors before.

"Yes, very nice. I'm wanting to stop by a bookstore on my travels."

"Ah, didn't know you had taken up reading." Did last night happen or did I just dream it.

"I haven't, I just have some questions I need to ask the lady that works there," I can tell by his reaction that he really wants to know what questions but isn't going to ask.

I don't know what he is up to, but I feel this all isn't because he wants to spend time with his disrespectful daughter.

"Ok. I wouldn't mind going to a bookstore myself actually; I'm in need of a new book."

I know he is saying that so he can have a better understanding of why I am wanting to go, and what questions are so important, that I would put myself out there and go to somewhere that I would never have been seen dead in, on my own.

"I don't think they will have what you want there, all the books are very old," I try to put him off, just so maybe he will wait outside or, fingers-crossed, go home.

"Even better," he smiles.

We finally get to the shop. It felt like the longest walk of my life. I do love my dad but he's not an expert at having a conversation with his fifteen-year-old daughter. He tried to ask me about boys, which got very awkward and uncomfortable for the both of us.

The shop appears to be dark inside; the closed and open sign doesn't seem to be there either. I turn to my dad to say it's best that we go, but before I can even get the words out, he's trying the door.

"Dad! What are you doing? It is clearly not open?" Well, the door is unlocked, and no one is in. Are we breaking and entering if we didn't actually break?

"Hello, any one in? Door was open, are you closed?" he calls. Nothing.

"I don't think anyone is here, we should go before we get in trouble."

I can't believe my parents thought I would steal when my dad is the one that has just welcomed himself into a possibly closed shop.

"Come on then, let's go," he says that while going up to the counter and peering into the back; is it just my dad's words that do not ever match his actions? It worked, because the lady from the other day comes out in another odd outfit; a dark blue flowery dress that I can only describe as something an older person with no taste would wear and a lovely (not lovely) brown cardigan, she has very weird taste. She is a very mysterious character and I think that if I had to guess her age, I'd say she wasn't far off one hundred.

"Evening. Sorry to bother you, is your store open?" my dad asks in a very posh accent, may I add.

"Yes, dear."

Me and my dad exchange looks, before I walk towards her, questions already forming on the lips.

"Hi, I didn't quite catch your name last time; mine is Adalyn and yours?" My dad is still watching me, waiting for my questions.

"Adalyn! What a fetching name. Mine is Read, Esther Read."

"That's my dad, Jerry Beckett." They both nod to each other as a silent hello, which adults seem to do a lot, especially my dad.

"I was just wondering if I could ask you some questions," I turn to face him, "while my dad looks at your books," he hurries over to the bookshelves, realising I caught on to his plan. "It's about that book, it is empty and I'm not sure what I should do with it."

"It is not to read as I said before, it is to protect. The book will answer many of your questions when the time comes; I can say no more, other than to keep it in safe hands."

"But when will that time come? Do I have to watch it? An attractive book it may be, but it's very pointless if you can't write in it or read it."

"My dear, not all books have the same purpose; some are special."

"But, why me, why did you give the book to me? Surely, other people have been in here, if not to buy a book but out of curiosity."

"Because the book is meant for you, I can tell, I know it," she starts to walk into the room at the back of the shop.

"I promise all will come clear, I can say no more. I have already said too much. Don't worry, don't panic, just believe you will find the answers; that's all you can do for the time." I turn around and come face to face with my dad.

“What are you doing! You just scared me half to death; why are you right behind me!” I know what he is doing, listening in to the conversation that he won’t ask me about.

The walk home consisted of my dad looking at me every so often with wide eyes, hoping I would spill all of my conversation with Mrs Read. He can stare all he wants, I’m not telling him. He’ll think it’s silly, and I’ll never hear the end of it; he’ll bring it up wherever and whenever and he may even make me take it back because, to be honest, it wouldn’t surprise me. The whole conversation I had with the woman and just the situation in general, is weird. How can a book answer me, and an empty book is even less likely, as there is nothing I can search for, unless I want to look at endless emptiness.

Chapter Three

I lay on my bed, the window wide-open, letting in the fresh warm air. I can hear the birds talking to each other, I can see the clouds slowly moving, making way for the dazzling blue cloudless sky, showing off the sun's bright rays. I take it all in, feeling a sense of calm. I take a few deep breaths inhaling the freshly cut grass scent that has wafted into my room, mixed with the tantalising aroma of food my mum is cooking that made its way up the stairs and filled the air. I feel patient, like anything that is troubling me has been pushed out of my mind, replaced with happiness; it is a wonderful feeling.

It turns out my dad did have something to share with me, and that was a job for myself. Unfortunately, he thinks it will give me the opportunity to grow and be ready for when I leave school and be in the real world. Not that I go to proper school, anyway. I am home-schooled by a very pushy, bossy woman called Mrs Fleetwood, posh and proper upper-class; looks down on you if a bad word so much as slips out your mouth, which is hard when 'crap' is not accepted. At least it beats going to a school full of teachers. It is quite tough though as I've not been able to make any friends, really. My parents have friends that have children, but they are quite a bit younger. I always get thrown into a room with them whenever we have a little gathering. I am like a babysitter, I just sit there silent at their little-child table, the chairs way too small for my bum, but I am forced by devil children to stay seated, while they all scream and cry like it's a competition who can be the loudest.

Anyway, back to the job. It's a Sunday job: greeting at my dad's friend's gardening shop, so it's basically me standing there for four hours, saying hello to people and handing out the occasional leaflet that says, 'Welcome, have you tried our brand-new cafe? Well, why not get 2 for 1 on our freshly made coffees and teas'. How I know about these leaflets is, whenever we go, we get one. I have about five hundred leaflets and the cafe has been open for a year now. I wouldn't call that brand new, I wouldn't even call it new. The only good side is I will get a bit of money for my troubles and if I do my very best and show Steven that I am up to the job, I can extend my hours and do a Saturday shift; my dad's words not mine, I couldn't think of anything worse. I hope Steven doesn't have high standards because he isn't getting it. I bet my dad has bigged me up telling him all stuff that he himself doesn't believe.

I start this Sunday, which is only six days away, that's not that long to prepare for my first day at a new job. I have a very particular routine that cannot be broken. I have also been told I am not allowed to call him Steven, and it's Mr Hunter to me. Not that I care because I will not be speaking to him, and hopefully, he will leave me be and let me do my job without him checking up on me every second, making sure I have said hello and handed out a leaflet to everyone that has walked through the door. I'm going to end up with a sore throat by the end of it and it will be all their fault.

I drag myself up from my soft bed to go see what Mum is making in the kitchen. I take a detour through the living room, to see what dad is up to because as I passed the door I heard a bang, then a word, I am not allowed to repeat, come straight after from my dad's mouth.

"What's that?" Dad is laid under a big wooden mess that I am guessing is meant to be a cabinet.

"What does it look like it is?" I can tell he is stressed; building is not his forte.

"To me, it looks like a pile of wood, maybe a massive Jenga?" I joke, which isn't appreciated at all; all I get in return is an angry look and a, "Go bother your Mum", so that is exactly what I am going to do.

"Hey, Mum, what's for food, smells good! Will it be long?" Mum stood giggling away at the noises coming from the living room.

"He's been at it for a while now; he's no closer to finishing, although he'll tell you different. I said I'll get Richard next door to put it together and that just made him even angrier. Thought I'd give him some room, so I baked a pie." I sit on the bar stool at the island eating some of the snacks my mum just placed down for me, knowing I won't stop going on about when the food is done if I don't have snacklets.

"Why can't he just accept defeat?"

"Your dad, accept defeat?" she scoffs. "That will never happen, he doesn't know what the words mean. He'll be at it, this time next week, knowing him." We both laugh and another bang comes from the living room and another word I cannot repeat.

Dad's always building things he knows he can't. Just about everything in this house has a screw or five missing from it, and will collapse if anything that has a bit of weight is put on top. We all just nod and smile when he has 'completed' something because, we know and he secretly knows, it is not complete. My mum has called our neighbour Richard around on a few occasions, when my dad's out to put all the missing screws in. I am sure that if my dad came home and was to catch Richard in the act, she would lie and say she was having an affair just so he never knows the truth. He tries but we all wish he wouldn't try and leave it to the experts.

"Jerry told me that you went to a bookstore to ask the lady about that book you got," she is looking into my eyes, no doubt trying to read them to see if I am going to come up with a lie.

"Yep," a simple reply, it will not go down well and she will carry on asking the questions, but if I share too much she will become concerned and go all motherly on me.

"And?"

"And what?"

"What's the book about?"

"It's not about anything. It's just a book, an empty book."

"Well, why was it given to you?" Inquisitiveness has taken over her.

"I don't know," I shrug, "she just wants to get rid of it, maybe I was the first person she saw and spoke to."

"Oh, bit weird to give a big empty book away for free. If my memory doesn't deceive me, it looked like quite an expensive one."

"Well, it is a bookstore. It is not that weird to have a book there that could have been there for a while, that she wants to get rid of. I don't think it is an expensive one really, close up it looks a bit cheap to me," I am hoping my answer will appease her.

"Your dad said he heard her say you have to protect it, and something about it answering your questions; what's that about?" I knew he was listening in on my conversation; he can't help himself, always suspicious of me.

"Of course, she is going to say that, she's a bookstore owner, she'll want me to protect it. She knew I was going to give it back so she just said anything for me to keep it. It's just a book, nothing special, as far as I am aware."

She does not look satisfied, but I seem to have stopped the questions. It is weird and I don't know what Mrs Read really meant. So far, the book has told me nothing and I do not know when the time will come, it will tell me anything. I am just as suspicious as my mother.

We all settle down for food around the table, which has been elegantly decorated with a colourful array of flowers, freshly picked out of the garden by me and Mum. Dad hasn't commented on the charming display we created, but then again, he is in a huff because he has been made to give up on the cabinet and Richard is coming around after dinner to finish where dad left off, which barely got started. He sat with a moody sign of defeated look on his face; it, surprisingly, has not departed by the delicious pie that is in front.

Chapter Four

It is my first day at work. I have been given a uniform that completely washes me out; it's not my colour at all. It is a light brown top with a green collar, with a matching logo in the same green. It is a little on the big side because they didn't have my size, as they didn't order it.

I have been placed outside, just by the door, so I don't miss any people and I've been told to smile and be good-natured, not lean against anything because it won't look professional. I hope I get a break; surely, I am not expected to work for four hours, without at least an hour's break?

First customer, time to put on a fake overly dramatic smile. "Hello there, welcome to 'Plants and more.'" Not a very decent name to me. Whoever thought of that name has no imagination. I bet it was Steven; he does not look like someone who would take some time to think of anything better than 'plants and more'.

"Here's a leaflet."

The woman takes a few seconds checking out the leaflet before taking an interest. "Have you got a brand-new café that is interesting? I knew there was one already, but two, wow. Do you sell different things in it?"

I am guessing she hasn't been here in a while.

“Actually, it’s just the same cafe, someone hasn’t bothered to update the leaflet or has too many to give away and is trying not to waste money by throwing them away.” I get given a dirty look by the lady and then by one of the employees, who happened to be walking by as I said that.

“Just hand the leaflets out and don’t speak,” the employee says in a snarky way. I bet she will tell Mr Hunter and think that I care.

I get asked a lot of questions, but I stand there ignorant. The employee, whose name is Carol. She had told me to not speak, so that I did. I just stood, handed out my leaflets and smiled. If I got asked anything and it didn’t go down well, it was funny to see Carol’s reaction; when I got a complaint and she came up to me to ask what I was doing, I told her I was just following what she told me to do. I got called a sarcastic silly little girl and was told to do my job properly or else Mr Hunter will be told, then she walked off with a smug smile. Not long after I overheard her talking to another employee, saying she isn’t going to tell Mr Hunter because, and I quote, “No one wants the job of greeter, they leave that to the strays. We are the professionals, we shouldn’t have to do the crappy jobs.” I don’t know where she thinks she works, but if by professional she means a professional snob then she hit the nail on the head.

I have made a new friend though. It is a lady called Jasmin and she does not seem to like Carol either, even more than myself. She is happy that she is now able to openly speak about her to someone else that can’t stand her, and her little crew that she has going on.

I am just collecting my stuff from the staff room when Mr Hunter and another staff member called Michael, stroll in.

“Hello, Addie.”

I hate being called Addie but Steven (I can call him that now, as I am not on duty) thinks it is acceptable.

“Hello, Steven,” he looks a bit taken aback that I have not called him his professional name, but he does not comment on it.

“How was your first day? Will you be returning next weekend?”

I contemplate for a few seconds just to leave him hanging, “Maybe, I will have to change my schedule.”

He laughs thinking I am joking; I am not.

“I’ll see you next week, Addie,” there is a hint of ‘please leave now’ in his voice so I quickly grab my bag and head out of the door.

I hope Michael is in trouble and getting a talking to. He is one of Carol’s followers and is quite frankly a moron. He follows Carol around with his mouth open, clearly obsessed with her. He hangs on her every word like she is spilling glitter. Why, I do not know because all I hear coming out of her mouth is a load of nonsense times-ten.

I am walking home because Dad wouldn’t give me a lift, even though I have been hard at work on my feet for hours and hours, which is his fault, I still have to drag myself home. All he is probably doing, is sitting in his chair reading the paper once again.

I take a seat on a bench by a river that is in the park down the road from my house. I am in no rush and I changed out of my uniform in the toilets at work, so no one will see me wearing that ugly thing. I watch as the parents shout at their children to come away from the water and the couples walking by, hand in hand, but not speaking, the groups of friends having a laugh, soaking in the sun by the river, their feet skimming the water. I am the only person on my own, I do not really know anyone around here. I haven't been able to make friends my own age because I have never been in the situation to. I cannot give someone a call and ask if they want to hang out.

An older man comes and sits by me, he has a flat cap on and is dressed old-fashioned with an old bruised walking stick.

"It's a fine day today."

I return with a nod and a smile, he does not take notice though, so he probably just thinks I am ignoring him; he is too busy watching a group of ducks heading down the river.

"I've been coming and sitting on the bench since I moved here, obviously not the same bench, I should add, as things are forever changing nowadays, but this same place watching the water travel." He's still watching the water, he hasn't turned once.

"Oh, I am sorry, would you like me to move on another bench?"

"No, don't be silly! It's nice to have the company."

"Do you always come here on your own?"

"Yes, it's not all bad. Are you waiting for your friends, dear?"

"No, I'm also here on my own."

He pulls out a bag of sweets and turns to face me, offering me one. I take one and we both sit in silence sucking on our hard-boiled sweets before he speaks again.

"I have six children and thirteen grandchildren, and not one of them have taken up my offer to join me. To the youngsters, I guess, it is a little lame to sit with your granddad watching the water; maybe one day," he sighs.

"Sorry, about us youngsters."

We talk for a while, mainly about his children and grandchildren. He also made me see things differently and how little time we have; time is taken for granted, he told me, imagination is key and that, although not all our dreams come true, we should never stop trying to achieve them and be the absolute best version of ourselves.

"Don't let anyone's opinions and thoughts on you, get you down either," he said. He is a wise man and he definitely makes you sit and think. I mentioned my strange encounter with the old lady and the book. I just felt he would have something to say that will help. At first, he was trying to think where the bookstore was and he had not seemed to have heard of it. He did say that he recognised the lady from my description, so maybe he knew her. He gave some well-needed advice though, after he pondered on the situation. He instructed me to go through the book again, in detail, because our minds can sometimes miss stuff that are of importance and if that does not work then wait; something will come, maybe it won't. He was interested in the situation though and said it reminded him of something, could have been a film he watched. He said it all sounds extremely exciting, even if I am on an endless roundabout. "Do not give up," were his final words before he stood up and went off to visit one of his children.

I reach home and am greeted by an empty house and a note reading:

'Adalyn,

We have gone over to the neighbour's house, they invited us around. We would have waited but didn't know when you would be home. Food is in the microwave, heat it up and make sure you eat it and don't waste it. Won't be long, don't mess up the house.

Love,

Mum xx.'

How am I going to mess the house up? It is Dad that leaves his tools and stinky socks around. Anyway, free house, that is amazing for me. I might throw a party. Oh, wait, I do not know anyone. Looks like it is just me, in front of the TV, with a bowl of soup, on my own.

I do not actually watch much TV. The stuff my mum and Dad watch are for old people that is not my kind of stuff, so this is a treat for me. I wonder what the old man's life is like. Is it weird to wonder what someone gets up to, what they speak about with their family. Do his grandchildren know about when he moved here, and that the place he has sat in the park since he moved here a while ago, was the place he first met their grandmother; would they go if they knew? He never mentioned if he told them or not.

I am enjoying this no-nagging situation. I have put my legs up on the sofa so I am in laying position, Mum would go ballistic if she saw because sofas are not for laying on, they are for sitting. "You have a bed for that," she says, if you so much as lift a leg up.

I must have nod off. I awake to loud knocking on the door and shouting through the letterbox. Why can't they just use their own key and not distract me. After many name calling from my parents, I soon realise that I have left the key in the door, which is the reason for the shouting.

"We have been knocking on the door for a good ten minutes, what the hell have you been doing!" So Dad's not in a good mood.

"Why did you leave the key in the door and ignore us knocking!" Seems Mum's not in a good mood either.

"Sorry, I was asleep; that's what work does to you, it makes you tired."

"Always using sarcasm as an excuse." Why does everyone think I am being sarcastic? I am being honest; work takes it all out of you.

"Ok, well, that was an enjoyable conversation, goodbye." I leave them to talk about me to each other, about how bad I am getting, and head upstairs to continue my sleep.

I had an amazing dream; I was in a field, it was greenery for as far as the eye can see, minus the sky, the trees were perfect, which I never thought I would ever hear my self say, but they were. The sky was a pleasing shade of blue with candy floss clouds, the air was glittering, like crystals were floating around, and it felt fresh. The sun was shining; it lit the sky and showed off in impressive detail just how stunning it is. It was just me, no one to be seen. It was silent. I felt like I had stepped into a work of art with its picturesque views. I have never seen anything like it and that is the first time I have seen it in my dreams. I wanted to see more, to explore beyond the trees, beyond the green, beyond my dream. I want to visit it in real life; it was so real but too unflawed to be real.

There are noises; I have just come into my bedroom and it sounds like someone is muttering. As soon as I close the door, the noises disappear, like I have startled them. I take a quick look around, suspicious and cautious. I do not see anything except for the book on my wardrobe. It is open; I do not recall opening it either, which is odd. Surely, Mum did not come up for a snoop and I can't imagine Dad bothering enough about the book to put his cup of tea down and come look. I feel the need to check any way.

"Mum, have you been snooping in my room?"

They both sat on the sofa, watching one of their weird programmes that looks very boring.

"Why would I?" She sounds offended.

"What about you, Dad?"

"Why would any of us go in your room; are you hiding something?"

"No, of course, I am not. It doesn't matter, I am going back upstairs. Enjoy your weird thing you are watching," I close the door before Dad can comment.

Why is the book open then, it makes no sense; it cannot just fall open. Has someone been in my room, someone I do not know, someone Mum and Dad don't know. I am a bit freaked out now; maybe they have rigged my room, that's why I can hear voices.

"Hello, if you can hear me, you aren't going to find anything interesting about me because my life is a bore. Find someone else." Who am I talking to; I have gone insane.

I take the book off the wardrobe to explore. Page after page of emptiness and dead ends. I go through it three times just in case that man is right, and my brain is hiding some details from my eyes.

All three times, I found nothing. Nothing at all, not even a single word. I feel I have been taken for a fool and the book does not mean anything. Should I wait like the old man also told me to do? Maybe I should.

I close the book and put it back on top of the wardrobe, backing away and not averting my gaze. I don't know if I am hoping for something to happen in front of my eyes, just so I have an explanation, or if I don't want something to happen, because no one has ever prepared me about what to do if a book that a woman I don't know, and met twice, and has a questionable choice of outfits, gave me, has some sort of power to open itself.

Chapter Five

I have been working at this pointless job for a good four weeks now, (I am really struggling to see how I have managed it) and home schooling is just around the corner. That means endless hours with my not-so-wonderful teacher Mrs Fleetwood. How she is a Mrs I do not know; her attitude should be enough to make any man run for the hills and never stop running. I feel sorry for her husband but at the same time I don't; surely he is under a spell.

My job has been a sham; Carol, the stuck-up employee seems to hate me even more than before, but not as much as she does Michael. Turns out, Michael was getting a promotion to head till person and not fired, unfortunately; and although that doesn't let him tell me what to do, as I am head greeter and the only greeter, so I am my own boss, but he thinks he can tell me what to do and boss me around. I don't listen but he still tries, it is laughable really how overconfident he is about it. He walks around with his chest puffed out, showing off his badge and I also caught him polishing it, although he did deny it when I brought it up, when I overheard him bragging to a customer. He also gave me a warning, which I did not take seriously seeing as he can't go giving out warnings, and I wouldn't care even if he could. On the upside,

Carol got jealous and hasn't spoken to Michael much since. I know she thought she was going to get it, which, much to mine and Jasmin's pleasure, she didn't even have a look in, ha-ha. Oh, how Jasmin and I laughed when she found out, I am sure I saw steam coming out of her ears.

I have not seen the old man since the first time we met; I was hoping to bump into him again. He had told me he was doing a five-thousand-piece jigsaw, oddly for myself, I have been wondering whether he completed it. He was really looking forward to placing the final piece.

Mum and Dad keep getting invites from the neighbours, to go to their elderly meals they keep putting on. Funnily enough, they just happen to have gone before I make it home from work. I sometimes feel like going around and saying, "Sorry, I am late", and see their reaction, but our neighbours are a bore, and I enjoy being on my own for a short while. It is funny how peaceful it can be when you don't have parents nagging in your ear every second or two.

I am back in the park again, in front of the river. It is my go-to place now after work, sometimes in the week as well, if I can be bothered to move out of bed. I am getting all my sleep in before schoolwork and endless nights of homework. I tip my head up so the delightful summer breeze can tickle my face and take away my worries. I feel something land on my nose. I open my eyes and go cross-eyed, hoping to see the suspect that has landed on the tip of my nose. It may just be that my eyes are now feeling weird and started to water, but I am sure this bug that is currently sitting on me, is the biggest, most colourful thing I have seen in my life, and no it's not a butterfly. I jump off the bench quickly, grabbing the attention of the strangers passing by. Everyone looks at me in disgust as I bat my nose at the area around me, like I am doing some kind of dance. A few other teenagers snigger as they go past me, silently judging my actions. I decide that is my cue to leave, waiting a few seconds for the group of girls to be at a distance, so I can't hear their comments about me.

I went past the bookshop the other day; I hadn't really thought about the book for the past few weeks. I thought about going in the shop, but it was closed. I guess, mysterious woman that never has customers to serve, deserves days off as well.

I get home, close the door behind myself, and rest on the door with my eyes closed, unaware my parents are home and standing in the hallway, staring at me.

"What are you doing? Have you been running? You're all red and sweaty." I had not been running, my fly swatting moves had me in a tizzy, causing my naturally rosy cheeks to go even rosier.

"Why do you never just say hello or how was work? Why is it always twenty questions with you?"

"Because you are always up to something," Dad comments.

"No, I am not, surprisingly, you just presume I am," my tone puts them off further questioning.

I walk past them, not looking them in the eyes and go get myself a drink. I down it in one. I slump down on to a chair and close my eyes; I am, then, pierced with looking eyes. I look towards the door, to the staring eyes of my parents, tutting away like expert tutters.

"Mom, Dad, just because I am a teenager it doesn't mean you have to stare at me twenty-four seven like an animal in a zoo."

"You never tell us anything." Mum's now parked herself on the chair next to me, but Dad's still watching on from the door.

"That's because there is nothing to tell. How can I be up to something when I don't have a friend or a life, for that matter? Most interesting thing that's happened to me today, is someone tried to rob something from the garden centre, but failed drastically."

I feel the silent pity from my mother take hold of me, "How is work?"

"Work is work, still as boring as the day I started. I have not been promoted to head greeter and nor shall I. I am more likely to find a million-pound laid on the floor outside, than get a sentence from Carol that isn't followed by a dirty look and a 'do your job properly'.

"When you think I am out after work, robbing old ladies or vandalising properties, I am actually sitting on a park bench, watching groups of friends pass by, listening in on their conversation about how the party they went to last weekend, was the best one yet," I hold on tight to the tears that are trying to escape, hoping they didn't notice that crack in my voice as I spoke, so I can keep my hard-core persona.

Dad joined, sitting on the other chair beside me, "If you would talk to us, we would know all this already."

"You don't ask."

"We are sorry." I feel a sympathy pat on the back. I don't know where all that came from, I guess I am sick of the judgment. I had to stick up for myself, inform someone I am not a bad person and behind my tough skin, I have feelings.

I spend the rest of the night downstairs sitting on the sofa with a pack of biscuits and a movie. My mum didn't even comment on the fact my legs are resting on the table, although I have been on the receiving end of her famous side eyes. I hear the yawns of my dad as he takes a long blink and starts snoring in no time. Mum soon follows so I take myself upstairs, taking the rest of the biscuits with me.

I got asked a few questions about the book I was questioning the lady about in my father's presence. I hadn't much to tell and I told them that. My dad offered to quiz the lady on it, but I turned his offer down. I told them I wasn't that interested anymore, which is true. I have become bored of asking a book questions, and scanning the book over and over, in case I missed something. I think I am part of some joke, a bit of humour at my expense to fill the lady's day, to take her mind away from the lack of customers. I am half expecting a knock at the door and for it to be her, asking if she can have her book back, now the humour has worn away.

I stare at the book on the top of my wardrobe as I finish off the last biscuit in the pack, adding the wrapper to the rubbish pile that has accumulated on my cabinet over time, due to my lack of interest in cleaning and out right laziness. I can't help but realise how the book is such a waste of paper. I've decided to take it off my wardrobe; it is tempting me to look at it for further inspection, even if I don't want to.

The moon light shines through my bedroom window, lighting up the book like a spotlight showing off the ancient looking pages in more detail. I never realised how much I like that old book smell; it is so distinctive and sort of pleasant. This is the longest time I have ever took notice of a book and even though it is empty, it still counts. I look in the corners once more and in the spine of the book, in case I missed some small writing, details of some sort, but like always nothing. I move from page to page, trying not to tear it. There must be at least eight hundred pages in this; they are quite large pages at that. Knowing my luck, I probably accidently missed the one page that says something. It will take me all year if I look at every page though, in much more detail than I am. Two hours later, the clock now reads 1 am and I decide to put the book back in its new home, so it can wait there until I become bothered again. I hear someone walking up the stairs, so I quickly throw myself under the blanket and pretend to be asleep. I wait for someone to open my door, but no one does.

Chapter Six

The next morning, I wake up to loud clutters downstairs. I put on my dressing gown but straight away I regret it, as I feel like a baked potato. The sun has heated my room up like an oven, but I am the sort of person that wears old pyjamas because they are comfortable, rip in the trouser leg or not. I just know that if I go down and Mum sees what I am wearing, my comfortable sleepwear will be straight in the bin. I go down to see who has woke me up at 9 am, which is practically the middle of the night, so it should be made illegal for people to be awake.

"What is all that noise, you do know I was upstairs, sleeping."

Mum pops her head out from the kitchen cupboard, flustered, "Just doing a clean out. Your Dad's in the living room having a look through that book of yours. It's just empty, isn't it? Crazy why someone would give you that for no reason. Why have you got your dressing gown on, its twenty-five degrees!"

I rush into the living room and pull the book out of my dad's hands before he can say a word. "What are you doing! Why, when I said to leave it, you don't?" I give him such a fright; he jumps spilling his tea all over his trousers.

"What did you do that for? Get me a towel, it's hot, this, you know. You don't half do stupid stuff."

"Well, leave my stuff alone then," I hold the book close to my chest like it holds my deepest darkest secrets that I don't want to get out.

"You shouldn't have made me curious then, you know I like a good book."

"It's not your sort of book though and it's not yours, you should ask before taking."

"Calm down, Adalyn. I am only looking in it, I'm not shredding the pages. It is a stunner though, isn't it? Definitely one of a kind that, can't imagine it was cheap. You can't expect me not to ponder on it." Ok, I can't, doesn't mean I want him snooping in my bedroom when I am asleep.

"There isn't anything to look at I've said, if I've looked more than once and not found anything, what makes you think you will."

"Fine, have it your way. Where are the biscuits, I went to get one earlier and they were gone."

"Mum ate them."

I run upstairs with my book strapped in my arms. I hear Mum in the living room telling Dad she hadn't had a single biscuit and blaming him for eating them all. I hide the evidence and dust the biscuit crumbs that still lingered from the night before, off my bed, and got dressed for another fun-filled day of doing nothing at all. I take my book outside on to the back garden, swerving my parents; how I managed that baffles me. I even managed to walk right past Mum, without her seeing me.

I sit on the floor behind a bush, so I am hidden from view. I check the book for tea stains; none that I can see, luckily. I am willing to forgive my dad for taking my property, seeing as I did make him spill tea all over himself.

I had a crazy dream last night. I was falling through the sky, I just kept falling. It felt like I was awake, and it wasn't a dream; I was reaching my arms out when I wanted to. I closed my eyes and inhaled the unknown air; it was pleasant to say I was falling through the sky. I felt all the emotions, and the fright at the beginning but then a sense of calm, like I trusted whatever was at the bottom, to catch me. I laid back and let the air carry me. My dream, then, soon took a sudden turn to me being at work, throwing bits of plant at Carol, until eventually she was buried in it. Strange but also not such a bad idea to use at work when Carol is on one.

It is not the first time I have had a dream somewhat like that. On the day I got given the book, I had a dream I opened the book and someone was speaking to me, asking for help and then I felt I was falling but I couldn't see anything, it was just dark; all I could feel was the air brushing against my skin, then I woke up.

Imagine if the book is magic. The whole situation gives out similarities of the start of a magical film. I shouldn't give myself such false hope; magic isn't real, apparently.

I hear my name being called, but I am going to take it upon myself to ignore it. I'm too lost in thought to go help clean the cupboards.

"Adalyn, I can see your leg behind the bush."

I move it quickly, like maybe, possibly, they will forget they saw it.

"Why are you sat behind the bush, we have seats. Why are you hiding on the floor?"

"Because Dad, I wanted privacy. Do you see me asking why you have those god-awful shorts on; no, so leave me be."

"Well, thanks to you, I got tea all over my other ones."

"You have other ones, why put these on? It's embarrassing. The neighbours might see you wearing them."

"Give over, or you're going to boarding school for being rude to my shorts. Get off the floor before you get grass stains all over your trousers, because then you will have to go put some of your dodgy trousers on, and no one likes that."

He goes away, laughing to himself, like he said a joke that was funny. His shorts are even more awful from the back; who in their right mind goes into a shop and sees bright pink shorts with palm trees all over and thinks, 'that's a great buy'. I bet my dad is the only person to contribute to the sales of these shorts.

It is such a gorgeous day today; the sun is shining the brightest it has all summer. The sound of children playing in the park not far behind our house echoes through its surroundings. Not a gust of wind in sight or dad's shorts and I may be wrong, but I could have sworn the book just shook.

I back away in caution, almost falling backwards into the bush. I don't even know what I am backing away from, because I am not one hundred percent sure it did shake.

It did it again! It definitely did, this time. If it does it again, I am afraid I may end up fully in the bush behind me.

I lean forward and place my hand on the book, like that is going to do something, awaken the beast or I don't know; what if someone pops out. How am I going to explain that one to my mum and Dad, 'oh hi, parents, this is my new friend, they just popped out the book, no biggie.' What if an evil person pops out; I could sit on the book, keep them in.

Wait, what am I even on about? Why would a person just come out of a book. It probably didn't even shake; my eyes are probably playing tricks on me, seeing as I was woken up at the crack of dawn.

I am just going to open the book, confirm my fears aren't true; the book is just a book, just one big purple unexplained book, which now reads 'enter' on the first page. Nope, closing the book, that wasn't there before. Someone's going to pop out. What about the other pages? Should I look? I am scared.

With a shaky hand, I turn the pages, preparing to throw the book a safe distance if anything happens. Still blank, except page one.

"Enter, what does that mean. You can't enter a book."

Everything is blank.

Chapter Seven

I am falling, falling through cotton candy clouds and crystal blue sky. There's nothing to grab, I am just falling, just like in my dream, except I have no hope this time. I can't see anything at the bottom, ready to grab me. I am not floating nicely like a feather or greeting any birds as I pass them because there aren't any. It is just me, falling with no parachute. I am going to die.

I approach the floor and prepare for my not so adequate landing, preparing to hear the crack my nose is going to make when it meets the ground, if I live long enough to hear it, that is. I try to shout for help, but I am too breathless to speak. I have this awful feeling in my stomach, like someone has just swung a bat and hit me square in the middle. This is it, I am a goner.

I say my final goodbyes in my head and wipe away the last tear that has fallen. Beneath me, what was once ground is no longer, it is now a massive green thing and the only way I can describe it is like a balloon.

Slowly sinking in the hug of the balloon, my heart rate lowers to a more normal pace as I swiftly get brought back on to two feet on a flat surface.

The balloon has gone and has been replaced with the greenest grass I have ever seen. It feels like grass, it smells like grass and looks like grass. Have I fallen asleep, because I was just literally in my back garden and now, I am here. This is not my back garden and I was just falling through the sky and came to terms with death or the breaking of my face. Confused is a complete understatement.

My surrounding is just grass and trees for as far as the eye can see. I find myself holding on to the smell of the freshly mowed grass, just for some similarities to my last surroundings. All I can do is stand there as my legs are still jelly. Is it worth calling out because I cannot see a single soul?

"Hello, anyone here? Mom, Dad, you there? Is this a joke because it is not funny. If it is because I slated your shorts, then you have gone a bit too far, even for your standards."

I try and get past my jelly legs and set off walking, where, I don't know. It may not be wise going into the trees unattended, but I am going to do it anyway, because after all, this is a joke, right, or a dream; either way, this I know, it is not reality.

I reach the edge of the forest, taking a quick look behind me just in case someone reveals their identity; then I take my first step in to the unknown.

The trees look like they are waving, but there's no wind. I feel uneasy but also very welcome. I hear the snap of a stick; I freeze, I don't want to walk into the hands of a bear or whatever animal is lurking in this forest, but to my luck (if I can call this whole thing luck) it's just the twigs under my feet, snapping as I step on them.

I carry on walking, still with caution, but also holding onto the thought that this is not real, I can't be hurt. I can hear birds tweeting above and feel the chill of the shade under the trees. The path is long and winding; I have not yet reached a dead end. There is something mystical about this forest; the wonderful plants beside the path are bright and colourful. The leaves of the trees shimmer in the sun, and there is no half-eaten food laying around or burnt patches on the grass, where someone took it upon themselves to start a fire, for no good reason other than ignorance.

I am still expecting my dad to jump out and shout, "ha-ha" in my face, "that's what you get for dissing my shorts," and when he does, he will get a swift kick in the leg for his troubles. I will cut his shorts in to tiny pieces.

"Dad, if you can hear me, as much as I adore this forest, I would like to go home now…to the comfort of my home. How did you make me fall from the sky?"

Part of me knows this isn't my dad's doing and the other part is really hoping it is, then it will (sort of) explain why one second, I sat looking through the book and then the next second, I am falling through the sky.

Wait, no, I can't have gone through the book; that is mad, even for me. I stop once again, remembering what went on. I sat on the floor, words appeared on the first page, I read them, and then next second I am here; that's all I remember. I can't do this, nope, it's not real, it can't be real, this isn't real, I am not here.

"Someone help me, please." I wait for a reply, not sure I want one. I have to turn back, maybe I will get sucked back into the sky and out the book? Yeah, surely.

I turn back around, heading towards the open land. Nope, I cannot, I've got to carry on going. My fingers are currently massaging the temples on my head. I have a stress headache, my mouth is dry, and I can feel the ache in my chest that has been caused by the unknown. I never wanted my parents to pop out from behind a tree as much as I do now, and ask me twenty questions.

I follow the path, it's the only logical thing to do at this moment in time. I can't come up with a more sensible thing. I think I will practise some breathing techniques, in and then out, in and then out. I feel better already.

I'm face to face with a tree, the largest tree I have ever seen and in the tree is a door, and there is no other direction to take. All the trees are so close together, it would make it impossible for myself to squeeze in between them. The door is small, much smaller than me, but a fetching shade of summer yellow and the handle is an attractive gold knob, it is all well and good but I haven't the faintest, what's behind that door. I might open it and be murdered on the spot. It could be home to someone that is not so welcoming to intruders. I think I will knock first, hopefully the owners are helpful. No answer, the knock sounded hollow.

"Hello, any one in? This may sound weird, but I don't know where I am; maybe you could help?" still no answer, just my own voice echoing in the air. I place my hand on the handle and slowly open it, crouching down so I can take a look through the crack in the open door before going in. It is just green, once again. I open the door fully and take my first steps in or shuffle should I say, as I can't really walk properly with my knees bent.

I have never seen something so magical in my life; I stood in awe of the incredible surroundings. I currently stood on top of a super high hill looking over at a town that looks like a place anyone would love to live in. The houses are all multicoloured but not scattered around, they are neatly placed in groups. I see little dots moving around that I can only presume are people, I am so far up. The cotton candy cloud vibes stick and the sky has a wonderful ombre of blues going on. I can smell strawberry bubble gum which gives me so many throwback memories of when I was a child, hiding my bubble gum from my parents by shoving it all in my mouth. My eyes linger on a building that's quite a distance away, but so grand it's hard to miss. I must look like a fish out of water right now; my mouth is just hanging open. I've had to wipe away the dribble that's made its way down my chin several times. I feel excited to explore but nervous; the pain in the pit of my stomach has not lifted, and I can't stop thinking about what I am going to say to someone, once I get down off this hill. To say I am in a tizzy, is an understatement.

Chapter Eight

I restart my journey by walking down this dreaded hill. Now, I am not a person that particularly likes hills neither walking up them nor walking down them. I once slipped on my way down one, when on an outing with my parents. I vowed to never step foot on one again, but seeing as this is my only way off, and seeing as when I turned around after going through the door, I realised it had magically vanished, I don't think I have much option, do I?

I have my flip-flops on and having a mare of a time with them. One slipped off as soon as I set off and since then I have spent a hell of a long time putting them back on. They really aren't suitable for hills and neither am I.

My plan is to go to the nearest person and ask them what I should do, where am I, and whatever else springs to mind at that point in time. I am going to turn into my parents and ask all my questions straight away, fire them out.

I am approaching the end of the hill and I have put my serious face on, because let's be honest, with what I am going to be saying I have a very slim chance of anyone taking me seriously.

"Hello, excuse me, man with the hat on."

I grab the attention of a man wearing a beige hat, sort of like one an old man would wear. I am sure my dad has that exact one. He is also wearing a trench coat in this weather; he must not be feeling the same weather I am as it is really warm. He does not look me in the eye. In fact, he lowers his hat even more over his face so I cannot see him much.

"Yes," he says, under his breath.

"Where am I? You see, I am in this weird situation right now; I just sat in my garden at home," I am waffling, "next second, I am flying through the sky almost dying and then walking through a tree."

I cannot see his reaction, but the hesitation says it all. "I can't help you, sorry."

"But I just need to know where I am."

"I said, I can't help you," he rushes off not giving me a second glance or a glance at all, he sounded extremely annoyed with me.

I move on to my next victim, a woman with rosy cheeks and a perky aura. She is actually approaching me first; she probably overheard my awkward encounter with the man and stopped to give me a sympathetic smile.

"You ok, sweetie, don't listen to him, it's that time of the month, he changes into an Octopus; you know how it is. I am Gertie."

It takes me a second or two to realise what she just said, "Wait, what?"

"His whole family, from generations, got cursed by a Witch because they can't keep their noses out of any one's business. Their own fault really, if you ask me, nosey parkers and gossipers. They stuck their nose in the wrong fire at this time and got it burnt that taught them. Anyway, enough about him, I overheard you saying you don't know where you are, or how you ended up here. I think I may be able to help you."

I take in what she is saying, but the whole octopus thing is completely playing on my mind. "How can you help me?"

"I've seen the goings on, I've walked these streets many times. I am not as young as I look, you know. Go on, take a guess at my age, I promise I won't be offended."

Even though she says she will not be offended she may possibly be lying, so I rein back one to fifteen years. "Sixty?" I say, hesitantly.

"Ha," she laughs out loud causing everyone in the surroundings to turn and look, "try adding a two in front of that and then some."

"You're over two hundred!" I say, in disbelief.

"Is the grass green?" The grass is, in fact, green and I am amazed.

"You don't look that old."

"Old? Pfft, I am in my prime dear, I have many more years before I am classed as old." I don't have anything else to say. For once, someone has rendered me speechless; there is a first for everything. Not even octopus man did that.

"Would you like my help or not?" she says it like I am the one who diverted the conversation to her age.

"Any help would be fantastic at this point in time."

"Follow me then, and I will lead you to your destination. I will also tell you a little bit about who we are if that's okay with you; don't usually get guests."

"That's more than okay with me, lead the way," I welcome her friendliness with open arms. I just hope she is not leading me to a sudden death.

We start to walk; where, I don't know.

“We are Tandalet, the place where the impossible is possible.” We then pass people with horns and someone who just melted into a puddle in front of my eyes, and no one batted an eye. He then got straight back up and carried on walking, like it is normal to just suddenly melt with no explanation. Children are jumping into massive bubbles, floating off in the sky and then coming back down to earth and popping them. “We are proud of our home. We built it from the ground up, we created the seas, the trees, what you see, we did it all.”

“It’s heavenly, I can’t lie. Back home is nothing like this, but I can’t help feeling like I am in a dream.”

She pinches me rather hard on the arm. “Ouch, what was that for.”

“You’re not in a dream, you are definitely here.”

“But I sat in my garden, next second I am falling through the sky and then I was caught by a massive green balloon,” I sound like a broken record.

“You will soon realise you will never get an explanation to the most complicated of situations.”

“But surely…”

The lady interrupted, “So there’s no point in asking.” I drop the questions about how I got here even though I have a million and two more questions to ask.

“Where are we going,” surely, she can answer one; it is simple, I think.

“We are going to the Queen; I think she may want to hear about your visit. It’s somewhat rare to have guests.”

“There’s a Queen?”

“Of course, there is. We would be all like headless unicorns if we didn’t have a queen, just running around and no idea what we are doing." If there are unicorns here, I may die of happiness. My inner child will come out and I do not know if I will be able to contain it.

"There are unicorns, please tell me, there are unicorns."

"Of course, there are; what sort of place do you live in that doesn't have unicorns. Go near any tree and you will see at least two."

Oh my! "I came through a forest and saw no unicorns."

"In Twiddlestone, you won't see any unicorns, they don't hang around there; too many Mymths in the grass, they don't get on."

"What are Mymths?"

"Mymths are tiny little creatures with super sharp teeth, they love to eat unicorns. You have so much to learn, unfortunately though, we have reached our destination."

I look up in front of me and there is a house, a big house at that, the colour of soft green and two doors on the front bang next to each other. A long path leads up to it with large black gates shielding, and two guards stood on either side.

"It's very pretty."

"Isn't it just."

"How come the Queen lives here and not in a castle?"

"Because a royal doesn't need a castle to rule."

Roses run up the side of the building, defying gravity. The windows are not in line with each other either, they are dotted everywhere making it abnormal, not a house I would stumble across back home.

"Let's try and get past these guards, then."

We walk up to the gates, making the guards stand tall, inspecting us from under their hats.

"I've got a girl here," they look my way, so I give a small awkward wave, "as you can see, she's not from here. I am not sure if the Queen knows about our guest or if her presence is known and expected, but I know the Queen will want to see her."

The guards give me another quick look, then go in on their own little conversation between themselves. Gertie gives me a shrug of the shoulders and turns back to hear what they have to say.

"We will have to speak to the Queen; we can't go letting any old person in."

"Excuse me," I go up with my hand up like I am wanting to ask a question to the teacher, "like Gertie said I am not from here. I haven't the faintest how I got here; in fact I sat in my garden looking in a book that was given to me by a Mrs Read. Unexplained, may I add, then next second, I am talking to a man that is turning in to an octopus."

The two guards go back in their huddle and have a quick whisper again.

"Mrs Read, you say." I am getting somewhere, finally!

"You didn't tell me that one, you silly sausage, makes more sense now," Gertie has chimed up, slapping her leg like she just remembered something she forgot.

"Yes, I said Mrs Read, why does it make more sense?"

"Well, Mrs Read is not going to hand the book over to anyone, is she?" she says this like I should know. Haven't I just said she gave the book to me unexplained.

"I don't know really, she didn't tell me a single thing. I just went to pick my mum a book and then get handed a massive empty one that I think I may be inside."

They open the gates and usher me inside. One of them throws an arm out in front of Gertie as she tries to enter.

"I will take you to the Queen, newbie. Sorry, Gertie you won't be able to come, just the girl for now."

"Why can't she come," I feel like I have a friendly connection with Gertie now, I cannot lose her at this crucial time.

"She's not got a reason to, has she," they close the gate leaving her standing there arms crossed and an angry look on her face, like a kid that's been refused sweets.

"Sorry," I call out.

I hear her arguing with the guard that has stayed behind, but he doesn't budge.

We stop outside the door and he throws his arm in front of me.

"These doors are the pain of my existence," he scratches his head, one eyebrow raised.

"How can a door be the pain of your existence," I asked.

"One of these doors lets you in, the other sends you back out. It changes each time; you'd think I'd have a knack for it by now but no, they clearly want me to suffer."

He stands in a thinking position for a little longer before selecting the door of choice.

"After you," he says ushering me through the door, "Ah yes, the right door. There's a first time for everything."

I look around at the interior. The floors and walls are marble in the grand hallway. And only a small table in sight. The same marble carries on up the heavenly set of wide stairs that are bang in the centre of the room. My feet hurt thinking about even walking up those stairs.

"Wait here, I need to see if the Queen is prepared to meet with you." The guard goes into a room to the left of the front doors.

I wait rather impatiently for him to come back, whilst checking out how spotless this hallway is. No pile of shoes by the door or dirt been dragged in from outside.

Who is this Queen, I imagine her to be very posh and snooty. I bet she is just like my home schoolteacher mixed with Carol; it doesn't sound too promising.

Moments have passed and the guard comes back out the room, closing the door behind him very gently as though to not wake a sleeping baby.

"The Queen has allowed your visit and requests that you meet with her in the living quarters," he said sternly. Why not just say, "She said okay, go in that room", much simpler if you ask me, not that anyone did.

I am not nervous; if anything I am eager to meet her royal highness. If anyone tells me what I need to do, then it's got to be her; unless she puts me in a dungeon for trespassing. The Queen sat on the sofa drinking something that may be tea or coffee, maybe hot chocolate. I know though that it is something hot, given that steam is coming out of the cup. The living area is, well, a thing of beauty also, I feel like I don't have a bad thing to say about anything I have come across on my journey so far. Everything is just simply taken out of a painting.

Her back is to me and she has not yet greeted me or turned around. I am tempted to talk first, but I don't want to make a bad impression on my first day, because I don't know if I am allowed to talk first. Imagine getting in trouble in the first few seconds.

"Hello, dear, sit please," she has finally turned around. Her hair is long and blonde, her eyes are the deepest shade of brown and her dress is long, baby pink and flowery, I love it. "This all must be very weird for you. I can't imagine what is going through your mind right now; tea?" she pours me a cup anyway, not waiting for my reply and hands it to me. I take a sip and straight away I regret it; that surely isn't tea. I am not going to be able to swallow it. "I bet you have many questions; shall we start with introductions." I pretend to drink more tea so I can try discreetly to spit it back in the cup. "I am Queen Tolstem of Tandalet, but I think we should be on a first name basis. Call me Yvonne."

"Er, hi, I am Adalyn." I am feeling very fidgety. I attempted to crack every finger on my hands multiple times just for something to do.

"Adalyn, you have come from so far away. I have in fact been waiting for you. I put my guards on high alert waiting for you." Oh no, am I going to end up in the dungeon, shall I run? She senses my fear because she gives me a warming smile to sort of ease my panic. "You know Mrs Read, yes?"

"Well, not really, we are more acquaintances. She gave me a book and didn't tell me a single thing as to why."

"Mrs Read is a very clever lady, do not doubt her reasons."

"I hate to be rude, but I am not from here. I have not a single reason to trust anyone from here. I still think this is some strange dream I am having and that's why I am not losing my head right now."

I take another regretted sip of my tea due to forgetfulness, and I have no choice but to swallow it because she will see. I had completely forgot about the vulgar taste with my mind being elsewhere.

She takes a seat next to me and puts a hand on my shoulder. Her tone of voice changes, its more straight talking and sympathetic than before.

"I get it. Well, I don't get it as such, because I have lived here all my life but haven't we all been put in a situation we have no idea what to do in. Just the other day the fairies did a blossom explosion prank, I had no idea how to deal with the fairies' new rebel attitude. I sat them down and spoke to them, but I could see it was going through one ear and out the other. I may as well have spoken to that door over there, it might have listened more. I promise you there is always a reason for change, and you are here not by coincidence but because we need you."

I sit silent, just pulling expressions, like I have smelt something bad. She is giving me time to process, she pours herself a fresh cup of tea, no longer having eye contact with me, but facing out the window.

"Is this real?"

"This is as real as you want it to be."

"What about my family?"

"I don't know how time works on the outside."

I close my eyes taking a long inhale through my nose. "Why do you need me?"

"You are welcome to take some time to come to terms with this."

My eyes are still closed as I speak, "I just need to know why you need me?"

"Very well." She stands up and paces back and forward by the window, still taking large gulps of tea. "People are disappearing, we don't know why. Another day, another home and business, empty. I don't know why; I am the Queen and I cannot explain any of this. Everyone turns to me for help and for once, I can't."

"They could have just moved," even my own words don't ring true to me.

"These people have lived here for all their lives, their families, for generations have lived here. We searched every other land, they are not there; we are desperate for answers. They are leaving family that are still here, and they don't know where they are. We have children without their parents; it's not good."

"Sorry if this sounds rude, but how can I help if you can't."

"Mrs Read was given the task to find the person that will be able to help; she has a sixth sense, more knowledge than a book could ever hold."

I want to ask if that is why she is called Mrs Read, or if it is just some coincidence but I hold back and ask a more appropriate question instead.

"So, she saw something in me."

"Possibly; she wouldn't hand the book to just anyone."

"Is it possible for me to take that moment to think what you offered up earlier? I need some fresh air." The room, although large, feels like it is getting smaller. I feel hot and lightheaded; this is just way too much to just get on with. I wasn't just handed a book, I was handed a responsibility to reunite families. I am fifteen, some would say I am barely even born.

I head for the door before she can reply and attempt to make an exit. I open a door and go through to reappear back in the building.

"This is a joke." I go for the other door given it is the only other possible exit.

"Why am I back in here again?" The other door has sent me back into the building once again; who decided it would be a clever idea to mess with a door. Third time lucky, and five or so minutes after my dramatic walk out, I am out the building. My mind is mushy peas, I can't even grasp any of the words that have been said, not even by myself. I think my mouth just went off on its own without my brain's permission.

I look by the gates and see Gertie sticking her head through the bars and having it pushed back out by the guards. She spots me and starts to wave vigorously.

"I waited for you," she shouts, making the guards jump.

I go along to her. Her face, although new to myself, is a friendly, comforting one and I need that in this mix of confusion and denial.

"Hi, Gertie," I have no energy to be perky.

"What's the Queen said," she is straight to the point, rocking toe to heel, with her hands behind her back, a look of urgency to know more on her face.

"I'll explain later, I just need to come to terms with it myself. We could go for a walk."

The guards let me out and Gertie hooks on to my arm as we stroll along. She doesn't speak and neither do I. I think she can see I am in thought not wanting a conversation at this moment in time.

We head towards the shops, which are all painted in bright light colours, different shapes and sizes, attached and detached, all close to each other; they line the paths in an s-shape. The street is filled with people peering into the shop windows, wondering if they should go in, if the shop holds the items they desire or if there is something in there that takes their fancy. Some have already ticked off their shopping lists and are now rushing home carrying their weight in shopping bags, pleading with their children to stay by their side and not stray.

"It's your own fault, you dropped your ice cream," one lady says to a blubbering child holding just a cone. "You shouldn't have been messing around, I'm not getting you another." This makes the child cry even more.

I watch them until they slip out of sight, down a path between two buildings, just a blob of ice cream left behind, slowly melting under the hot sun.

"You don't have to tell me but what happened."

I don't reply straight away. I watch the ice cream run down the cobble path until it comes to a halt by someone's shoe. They walk away unaware of the ice cream they just picked up.

I tell her what was said. She pulled a lot of 'Ooo, get you,' faces which weren't appreciated.

"This is a big deal, you know. These disappearances have rocked the land and I bet everyone will be ever so excited that they have brought someone in to help."

"Please, don't tell anyone, Gertie, I don't know what I am going to do; this is a big thing. Not so long ago, I thought I was in a dream or my dad was pranking me after I was mean about his shorts."

"It would be one big prank creating a whole land. Listen, you know that if you go ahead with this, I will be by your side no doubt, because who's better to help than a two hundred and whatever person." She gives me a nudge on the arm that almost made me fall through an open shop door. She is quite a strong lady.

"Thanks Gertie, but I haven't thought about what to do yet. It is a big ask for a fifteen-year-old that's just got here."

"I get it but think about it, yeah?" we walk in silence again and just keep walking and walking until we get to the houses.

The sun is beaming. I close my eyes for a second, just picture myself back home on the garden, sunbathing, hidden in plain sight from my parents.

"Ow." I stood on the back of Gertie's shoe, pulling the back off her foot.

"Sorry, I slipped," she crinkles her eyes, not believing my excuses, while attempting to put her shoe back on without stopping.

There is shouting, not far away from us, coming from one of the houses. I take it that Gertie loves a good snoop, she pulls me towards the voices, a big smile smacked on her face.

"Don't think I won't kill you with my bare hands, Uno," a lady and a man are standing in a garden, the lady is holding a sweeping brush, waving it in the sulky man's face. "You have hit a nerve for the last time, now clear off. Go on, scram you inconsiderate twit," she slams the door in his face. Next second a rain of clothes come from the top window, showering the man and burying him in a heap. "Take that, scum; I only asked you to take the bins out! What's so hard about it? Oh, hello, Gertie, smashing day, isn't it."

"Delightful," she shouts up, eyeing the large underpants that have just flew out the window, landing on top of the man's head.

“Not a grey cloud in sight, it’s a welcome change.”

Uno is scrambling around, gathering up all his possessions as quickly as possible, hiding the underpants under his arm away from the crowd now gathered. By the looks on their faces, they are regular guests to the man and woman’s show.

“A funny pair they are, and I don’t mean in a ha-ha way, they have the same argument every other day. Within an hour he will be back home, and it will be like the argument never happened.” The crowd has now disbanded, and Uno is walking away with a hand full of clothes, trying to scoop up the clothes he keeps dropping. He side-eyes us when he walks past, which wasn’t wise, he’s just tripped over a trouser leg because he took his eye off the ball and dropped all the clothes, once again.

As he scrambles around, the show now over, I take the opportunity to find out more about where I will be staying for however long. “Gertie, can you tell me some more about the land.” I am hoping details will help me come to terms with this whole situation.

“Sure, thousands of years ago our land was created. We had nowhere to go, nowhere to call home, until a man called Oaky Tolstem uncovered this empty land after years of looking. He moved everyone in and they built our land from scratch, brick by brick. It was not easy, but it was worth it in the end; just look at it, you’ll not find anywhere else like it. Oaky became the king and when he died, his son took the crown, many, many years ago. It goes on from there.

“Now, we have our Queen Yvonne Tolstem, also known as Tolstem of Tandalet. She’s kept us going and given the circumstances, she’s done a rather decent job at it. I haven’t a bad word to say about the Queen. If it wasn't for her family, we would not be here; we may not even be alive and we are all afraid that all the work will soon be taken away. I have actually lost some of my family myself, just gone. It's been months now, I'm not getting younger. I'd like to see them again, it's the first time anything bad has happened here. There was never any fear but now that's all we live in: fear."

She wipes away a stray tear, not looking in my direction. I know she is trying to hold back a stream of them, so I put my arm around her shoulders. I am not good at the whole cheering up thing but she smiled, so that's good enough for me.

"I just need to pick something up from one of the shops, fancy coming with?"

"Of course."

There is a corner shop not too dissimilar to one near my house but it doesn't sell chocolate and dodgy looking sandwiches. It's sweet and smells like herbal essence. I think this may be some sort of pharmacy.

"What does it sell in here?" I look around at all the stuff that I haven't a clue what they are, while Gertie goes to speak to the shop assistant.

My attention is diverted to a bottle filled with a turquoise liquid, softly moving in between its glass walls. I lean in closer; my head magnifies in the shimmer. Gertie has finished speaking to the man and is now standing beside me, also looking into the liquid.

"What's this?" My hand grasps the bottle for closer inspection.

"I wouldn't open it," Gertie's hand rests on mine.

"Why not, I just want to smell it."

"Because one whiff and..." I remove the diamond lid before she can say any more. I wake up on the floor to water running on my face and hair, making its way up my nostrils giving the feeling of having my head dunked under water.

"As I was saying, one whiff and you'll go nap time."

"Did you throw water on me?"

"How else do you think I'd wake you up?"

I stand up and shake like a dog, sharing the water droplets with Gertie. "Hey, what did you do that for?"

"How else do you think I'm going to get dry?"

So I just found out the people in this land share the same broad vocabulary of my dad.

The shop assistant approaches, not looking at us but the puddle on his shop floor and the shards of glass that are scattered around. The only remains of the once sleeping potion.

"I hope you have plans to clean that up, that's a slipping hazard, that is."

"Gertie was just saying about cleaning it, weren't you, Gertie?" I give her my best smile.

She replied through gritted teeth, but my selective hearing didn't pick it up.

"I'll wait for you outside while you clean."

I leave the shop just as Gertie is being handed a mop and brush. I also hear her getting a grilling for taking the water he was using to water his plants.

As I rinse my hair out, I hope today is the day the frizzy mess my hair turns in to when wet, decides to not make an appearance. A shake of the shoulder would have done the job of awakening me, not a face full of water.

Chapter Nine

"Please, can Gertie come in; I am sure the Queen will let her," we stand outside the house not accepting the guards' refusal to let Gertie in.

"It's not our choice to make, mam."

"Come on, I will say I got you in headlocks and tickled you until you let her in." I do the tickle motion with my fingers causing the guard to bunch his shoulders to his face, hiding his neck clearly thinking I am going to tickle him.

The guards are contemplating what I said. I can see it in their faces, so now me and Gertie are pulling our bottom lip over the top and pulling our best puppy dogfaces.

"Come on, you guys, you know me, what is old Gertie going to do, eh, cause a scene?" she looks at me when she says old because of my earlier comment.

"I've heard what you get up to, don't act innocent. Did you return that gnome to Mrs Ferbertal you claimed was yours but ran off from your front garden to hers?" I try not to laugh and keep the puppy dog eyes intact. "Go on then, but I tell you this, if we get fired, I will be after you Gertie, mark my words."

She throws herself through the open gate and plants a big kiss on both the guards' face. She did have to pull them down a few inches because she is not the tallest of people. They wipe her sloppy kiss straight off their faces. "If I knew you would kiss us, I'd have said no."

"Now, we just have to get through those ridiculous doors," I comment.

"Ah, yes, the prank doors. Did I mention Oaky was a prankster; the doors are just one of his little brain teasers." Can't say I am looking forward to uncovering the rest.

"Which door, then," Gertie responds by pointing at the right-hand door.

"It's an instinct." I trust her instinct and we go through the door.

"Didn't say it was a good instinct." We are back on the front again.

I choose this time, going for the same door as before hoping for the best.

The best didn't happen and once again we are back under the hot sun. The guards are having a good laugh watching us struggle.

"Maybe third-time luck," we go through the left-hand side door this time and I would like to say we got through, but we didn't.

"Right, I'm sick of this, let's just open the door and keep going through we got to get it onetime."

One more time, two more times, three more times, four more times and finally, eighth-time lucky. The guards are currently in fits of laughter on the floor.

"Maybe they don't want you in, Gertie," they shout across, as we finally make our way into the building.

"Right, what do we do, now?"

"Hopefully, the Queen is still in that room," I point to the door I once went through before, "if not, we will just wait, I guess."

We walk in the room making our entrance clear. The Queen still sat on the same chair she was in before looking out of the window.

"Ah, seeing as it is you that has come into the room like a herd of unicorns, I will let you off for not knocking and barging straight in; please take a seat. A pleasure to see you again, you too, Gertie."

Gertie looks like she is going to explode with happiness that the Queen knows her name. Her cheeks are all red and plump.

"I hope your return is good news."

"I'll help you. I am sorry for how I acted; it was completely wrong of me, but I just don't even know, I'm stuck for words. I can't get my head around this; I feel like I am going to wake up any moment and just laugh this all off, because, and I mean this in the nicest way possible, it's all just bizarre."

The Queen and Gertie are nodding in unison.

"Bizarre, yes, but I know how grateful the land will be and just know I am grateful also."

We sit and I would say drink tea but every time the Queen turned her back, I tip it into a plant and then she would refill again. I tell you this for a fact when I get home, I am making the biggest cup of tea you ever did see; I will enjoy every little sip.

All this chatting had taken my mind off home, I have not yet asked the questions of when and how am I getting home. My mum and Dad may be out looking for me now. I have been here a good few hours now. I can't help but feel bad for my parents not knowing where I am.

I haven't yet got my head around being here, I really do not think I will. If I leave knowing I did nothing to help all these people, I will forever hate myself whether this is reality or not.

My silence catches the attention of the Queen. "Adalyn, you must be extremely tired. You are welcome to stay here; we have a spare bedroom set up for you. Winnie," a lady quite tall, cropped red hair, appears at the door carrying some folded clothes in her hand. I am not tired one bit seeing as I have just stepped from morning to afternoon and basically just woke up a few hours ago. "Winnie, please take our guest up to her room."

"Yes, mam," she beckons me to follow her.

"I'll be here bright and early, Adalyn," Gertie says, as I bid goodnight and follow Winnie to my room.

"It's nice here, not like home," I try to make conversation with Winnie unsure how friendly she is or if she wants to speak to me.

"From a new eye, I bet it's something of a picture," her tone is cheerful, but I feel there is more to her words.

"Do you like living here?" I go to dig a bit deeper, hoping she will tell me something no one else here would.

"I do, I just feel...closed off; nowhere to visit except the same streets. I'm being silly, but I have always wondered what is beyond here."

"It's not silly. Why don't you look beyond?"

"No one in this land goes beyond this land and even if we could, my family come from a long line of loyal aides; we vowed to protect the royals, it's the only thing we can do. We are only allowed out at night; the sun makes us go up in flames. It's no fun being a walking flame unable to touch anything, speak to anyone, even walk for that matter."

"Has everyone here got some abilities, power of some sort?"

"Sort of. Your friend Gertie, well, her family lives for years and years way beyond any of us, she's seen it all. We have witches, wizards, people who aren't in that category but can do stuff others can't, people who are part animals. Rarely any one can do the same thing."

"Does everyone get on here? I imagine it being a tight knit community, well, minus the woman throwing her husband out on the streets."

We stop in front of a picture on the wall along the landing. "This is Maxim, the father of our Queen. He was murdered by a man named Heston."

"Why did he kill him?" I can't imagine anyone here hating someone else so much that they would take their life.

"Heston had a good heart, once upon a time. He is Maxim's cousin, unfortunately his parents died due to an illness that was going around at the time when he was only young, so he was brought up by Daxton and Barbetta, Maxim's parents and also King and Queen. Maxim and Heston were inseparable, wanted to be known as brothers, not cousins.

"Heston was the one that never showed any sign of greed or aggression but Maxim, he was the perverse. As a child, he would steal sweets from other children, using his powers to do so. The roles reversed. As they got older, Heston thought he would be king although not in direct line for the throne. He bragged a lot. It was and still is unknown, why over the king's son, he thought he would take the throne. The little boy with not a single bad bone in his body and the rosy red cheeks that would get pinched as he said good morning to everyone he passed on the street, turned in to a power-hungry monster. Of course, this wasn't seen in public; minus the bragging he was still an angel.

"Maxim outed him, the once hooligan turned good honest family man because he had so much love to give to his daughter, Yvonne, and wife, Mae. Heston didn't have a family of his own, but everyone knew he wanted one, he treated Yvonne like his own. Daxton died and Barbetta was no longer Queen. Maxim took over, much to Heston's dismay; you could see the fire burning in his eyes as Maxim was crowned. Not long after, Barbetta died taking a secret with her. Maxim said the secret was, Heston wasn't who everyone thought he was and that he was evil, the family had tried to hide it for so long and claimed he himself had to put on the persona as bad child to hide just how black-hearted Heston was. Heston vanished, that's until Maxim was brutally murdered as he slept, a knife through the heart, my grandmother, also his aide, said. A lot of people asked how did Mae not witness this. They did not share rooms; as Yvonne had night terrors, she looked after her, leaving him vulnerable and an easy target. Heston once again left, never seen since. There were rumours he died, but rumours are rumours and that's all they have ever been. It was known that Maxim's body wasn't seen by anyone except by my grandmother. It was his wish that if he was to die, he did not want his family to see him and if found by another, the aide was to sort him and that is it. Mae wanted revenge, she searched high and low for Heston until her death five years later. Yvonne was only fourteen when she was crowned Queen and nineteen when she was left alone, the only Tolstem left. She looked after herself with the help from us aides and the land, no husband and no children."

She shows me to my bedroom, leaving me pondering.

"Don't hesitate to call me if you need anything," she places the neatly folded clothes on to the bed and leaves the room.

The pyjamas she has left me are an acquired taste, a very old-fashioned nightgown it has a collar on it and everything. I don't really think I have much option, other than to wear it. It is either this or my clothes and that's not happening, sleeping in anything but pyjamas is uncomfortable. I put on my nightgown and get in to bed staring at the ceiling, begging my mind to switch off and have a burst of tiredness. I never struggle to sleep, naps are my thing.

After thirty minutes of trying, holding my eyes tightly shut, I look out the window. The sun is no longer there; it's been taken in and replaced with a glowing half-moon. I look closely at the lights dotted around the sky, they look like lanterns, they a delightful crimson red and I don't know if I am seeing things, but I am sure they have big eyes partnered with a small mouth. There are loads of them, just sitting there in a calm manner carelessly humming a tune I hadn't noticed earlier. I close my eyes and let the song tickle my ears, making my eyes get heavier and heavier. I slip back into bed and let the stress from the day take over.

Chapter Ten

I wake up to the sun peeking through the gap in the curtain leaving just a line of light across the floor. I didn't dream last night; well, not that I can remember any way. I did wake up a lot in the night though, looking around the room for some sort of normality. I do not move at first, I stay in bed staring at the same bit of ceiling I did last night, that's until I hear a knock at the door.

"Miss, are you awake, it's me Winnie. I have some food and clothes for you."

I sit up and run my fingers through my hair, trying to rid of the knots that accumulated over night.

"Erm, you can come in." Winnie enters carrying a tray and clothes laid over her arm, a big smile on her face.

"Good morning, Adalyn, I trust you slept well. I thought you'd be hungry and maybe want some clean clothes." She puts the tray down on the bedside table and the clothes on the shay lounge by the window. "I hope you like the clothes; I don't know what your style is, I took a guess."

"Thank you, Winnie,"

She nods and exits the room leaving me on my own once more. I don't feel that hungry, my stomach is still doing back flips; I could not eat even if I wanted to.

There is a bowl of porridge and a little pot of fruit with a glass of orange juice. Not even the juicy strawberries look appetising to me at this moment. I pull myself out of bed and go and inspect the clothes I have been gifted; not too bad, there's a flowery top paired with shorts. I can live with that and I will be happy to get this nightgown off; the collar is cutting off the circulation to me brain and it's very ugly.

I head downstairs holding the still full bowl of porridge and part drunk orange juice.

"Morning, Adalyn." Gertie pops out from nowhere.

"Gertie, you scared me half to death."

"Sorry, are you eating that porridge?" Her eyes are popping out of her head from the sight of my food.

"Nope, go ahead." She takes the bowl without a second thought, shovelling it in her mouth, not stopping for breath.

"I haven't eaten, been here a good few hours trying to persuade the guards to let me in. Winnie came out and rescued me, just in time and all. I was about to give them a duffing," she picks the rest of the orange juice up and downs it, "thirsty as well," she wipes her mouth on her sleeve and looks satisfied with her feast.

"Is the Queen awake?"

"Yeah, course she is, I'm not allowed to see her yet, she's still eating, don't want distracting. Winnie said I talk too much and it may be off-putting, so I got banned."

"Didn't they offer you breakfast?"

"Nope, I don't live here, do I, they won't feed me."

"Come on, shall we go in the living area and wait for Yvonne; I suppose she'll have a plan to share with us."

"Seen as we can't really do anything until the Queen is ready, fancy going and seeing the fairies? They should be out and about."

Of course, I want to see the fairies; does Gertie even need to ask. We go in to the back garden and it has the most delightful array of flowers Hydrangeas, Osteospermum, Crocosmia, Fuchsias, Campanulas, you name it, they have it and I see myself as a plant expert, thanks to my parents' love of gardening. They would adore this garden; it is a thing of glory that makes me feel at home. I admire the wide range of flowers as we make our way up towards the fairy houses at the back of the garden.

"Fairies are little devils but if you catch them in the morning, they are more peaceful. It's towards night-time they go wild."

We reach the fairy houses, some small, some tall, all-colourful just like the normal houses. They remind me of the fairy villages you can create in your garden by buying stuff from the shop. I love them.

There, a couple of fairies sat on the wall; I think they may be sunbathing. I was expecting to see their body surrounded by a halo of light like I've seen in pictures, sort of like tiny lightbulbs but although they do look like a typical fairy, there's no light. They see me and Gertie and start whispering to each other.

"Do they speak?" I ask Gertie, not taking my eyes off the fairies.

"They have a voice box, you know."

The fairies fly up in front of us, one has pink sparkly wings, the other has blue sparkly wings and matching dresses.

"We don't know you," I just about hear what they say.

“I’ve actually just arrived here.”

“Arrived from where?” I do not think they care where I have come from, purely based on their titters.

“She has arrived from another land,” Gertie has now averted their attention.

“Have you arrived from another land?”

“No.”

The fairies start whispering again and then turn back to Gertie, “We know you, you are that weird woman.” Gertie doesn’t look offended at all; in fact, her smile has not faded.

“Adalyn, Gertie, are you out here?” there is a distant call from towards the house that makes the fairies fly back into their houses.

“Yes, we are here. Seems the Queen has finished.”

We make our way back into the house again and into the living room. Yvonne sat on her usual chair, yet another pot of tea in front.

“I hope the fairies were polite, they do have an attitude problem at the moment.”

“They were friendly enough,” I say as I take a seat across from the Queen. I do not know where to look. I am locked in a staring contest with the Queen and she is yet to blink.

“What’s the plan then?” she finally looks away, splitting her eye contact between me and Gertie.

I let out a laugh, a mixture of nerves and confusion. “Wait, what. I haven’t got a plan, I thought you had.”

“We wouldn’t need your help if that was the case.”

I stand up, stumbling over my feet in the process. “I’m not quite sure what you expected, but I got here not even twenty-four hours ago. Do you think I came pre-planned?”

Gertie is staring at me eyes-wide, clutching on to the side of the chair, she looks like she is bursting for the toilet, but I know she is pulling that face because of the way I just spoke to her Queen.

"Maybe I did expect you to come into this room with some sort of plan," her voice is plain, no sign of anger. Her expression has not changed either. She's just sipping on her tea.

"You'd think the Queen would have a little something to go on."

"Well, I guess we both got the wrong end of the stick then."

"I guess we did," I slump back on to the chair.

My brain has just done that thing, when you try to admit defeat but it's like no way I'm still ticking away; I have a hidden gem, "I've got it."

"Got what," Gertie is still clutching on to the chair, she is probably expecting me to start ranting.

"An idea," the Queen's expression finally changes, just a little. I saw her eyebrows rise slightly, "so, I have seen inspector films on the TV."

"The TV?"

"Yes, Gertie, the TV, it's something we watch. Getting back to what I was saying, they always look for clues around the homes, what were they doing before they went missing, any signs of break-ins, that sort of stuff."

"And will that work, do these inspectors get their answers?" the Queen asks.

"Nine out of ten times, sure."

"Then you know what to do then. Will you be needing any assistance or equipment?"

"Not at this moment in time. I've got Gertie."

The Queen rises, placing her cup of tea on the table, "Excellent. I will see you when you return."

Do I dare to ask for a little more of a reaction than just a simple 'excellent.' As I get to the door, I realise Gertie is not following, in fact she sat stuffing her face with biscuits. She turns to look at me, cheeks cram-packed.

"Are you coming?"

"Sorry," she spits out biscuit crumbs all over her lap, ew.

After she has dusted herself down, she finally followed; not before filling her pocket though, with the leftover biscuits.

We didn't have a problem with the doors this time around, straight through our door of choice, which I think annoyed the guards when we told them. They seem to enjoy everyone getting stuck at the doors, even though they get stuck themselves, more than once a day, at that.

"Have you been kicked out by the Queen Gertie, for stealing all her biscuits," they nod towards her full pockets.

"At least I don't have to stand in front of the gates all day, you're just jealous because you can't eat any of these biscuits."

I dawdle between the shops again, ear wigging on conversations to find out if anyone else has disappeared.

"Could we go to one of your family members' house, check it out," I thought aloud.

"Sure."

I admire Gertie for keeping a level head through her trauma. I can't imagine what she must be feeling not knowing where her family is, she hasn't mentioned it since our chat but every so often I look at her and I can see tears brewing in her eyes and I feel this ache in my chest, sympathy clutching on my heart.

On route, I have heard a lot of gossip about the missing, none mentioning any recent ones though.

"She just vanished; poor Rosalyn was upstairs clearing away the washing went back down and she'd gone just like that, not even a goodbye. Of course, at that moment she thought she had gone out with her friends. Didn't think much of it. It got late and she hadn't come back and then obviously more people came forward saying the same thing. Mrs Teedys been gone a while she would not just up and leave, she loves her little shop. Called it her pride and joy. To me, I think she could do so much more with it, it's not the best of shops, if you ask me."

"I've heard a rumour they have got someone in to sort it all, from a faraway land they are saying. Apparently, the Queen has put all her trust in this newbie, can't say I have."

"I've heard about that. It's a young girl, someone said the other day she didn't look very happy to be here. I can't see her being able to help if our Queen can't. I think the Queen just wants it to look like she's actually doing something."

I hide my face as we walk past these gossiping ladies, unfortunately, Gertie is a well-known lady and catches their attention.

"Hello, Gertie, not seen you in a while. Been busy, have you," Gertie stops in her tracks, not happy to speak, while I duck into a shop doorway.

"Oh, you know, people to see, places to go."

"Have you heard about this girl that's apparently come to save the day? It's all ridiculous if you ask me, I bet you're not too happy that they have put an outsider on the case to find your family."

"I've met this girl and I can tell you this, she has a wiser head on her shoulders than most of us, especially the ones that stand around gossiping all day." I wish I could capture their faces, absolute picture-perfect moment. A mental picture will have to do. "Don't forget to shut your mouths, you'll catch dragon flies."

They strut away, ready to tell another gossiper about their encounter with Gertie, twisting the events for their own benefit.

"Thank you, Gertie. You didn't have to."

"Meh, I did, and any way I wasn't keen on them in the first place. A pair of haughty cows."

I can't disguise my smile; no one has ever stuck up for me before; it's weird. We get to a small house in a nice shade of pink and a thatch roof.

"This is it, my great-great-granddaughter's house."

It is really cute inside, a proper country house, even the bright yellow walls and the clash of colours don't make me want to grind my teeth, but it is cold and it's all musty. It feels lonely; you can tell the thing that makes it a home has gone.

"She's been gone a couple of months now, couldn't bring myself to come in before; you'd think I would have at least come into double check, but I knew. I was invited around, you see, but when I got here, no one was answering, I don't like using my key, so I left it at home. I went to go get it, got home and had the realisation they had been the next victims, couldn't bring myself to go back," Gertie goes around opening windows letting fresh air seep in.

We look for clues around the house, noting the pair of half-eaten sandwiches on the table and the full pot of tea on the stove with the two empty cups on the side. The door has not been broken and neither have any windows.

"Was the door unlocked when we got here? I wasn't paying attention."

"It was locked."

I try and think about the last inspector film I saw a few weeks back. I ask myself what would that moody inspector do.

"If we find one of the missing, I have a feeling we will find them all. This is so weird, how can someone get taken from a locked house...Gertie?"

She stood looking at a picture on the cabinet, a family portrait. I spot Gertie straight away, the biggest smile ever, complete and utter joy all over her face, her family stood behind her, all-smiling as well.

"I remember this day, I'd begged them to have a family portrait and they finally agreed. It was one of the best days of my life, all my family in one place enjoying themselves. My daughter, her husband, granddaughter, her husband, great-grandson and his wife," she points out each family member on the picture, "vanished first, from my house while I was in the garden picking some vegetables for our tea; the lot of them, just gone like that, no warning. I thought they were hiding from me at first…then my great-great-granddaughter and her little family, I miss them," I wrap my hands round her and shed a tear for her and myself.

"I can't imagine how you must feel. I have been away from my parents for not even a day and I miss them more than anything even though we haven't really been getting on."

“Take it from someone who has many years of life experience, seconds are valuable, days even more so. We shouldn’t let trivial things spoil relationships because then we hold regret and no one likes regretting.”

I felt that, in the pit of my stomach, those words, they spoke volumes. I break down. I have been here a day and already crying. When do I ever cry like this; Gertie has broken me well and truly.

We sit there together, letting out our emotions from our eyes and every time I try and control my sobs, more come out. Why does that happen, you are telling yourself not to cry but your eyes are like, nope, I am not stopping. I bet my face is all red and my eyes look like puffer fish. I feel like I could go to sleep now and have a long nap. Crying really takes it out of you, and I would do anything for a nap. I am already two naps behind already.

“We have got to pull ourselves together; we can’t sit here blubbing all day. We both look like we have been in a fight. Let’s do this for our families, so you can get yours back and I can return to mine.”

“Here, here.”

I feel like I should dust for prints, but I don’t have any equipment for that. I could go DIY style and walk round the room with some tape.

“Gertie, does your great-great-granddaughter have any tape,” she bobs up from behind the sofa.

“There’s nothing behind here to help us, what’s tape, when it’s at home.”

“I will take that as she doesn’t have any.” I wouldn’t know what to do anyway if I did get some fingerprints. It is not like I have a scanner; it just seemed like the right thing to do.

"I really don't think we will find anything here; shall we move along?"

"Come on, then," Gertie goes around closing all the windows she opened, which didn't alter the must scent, but I'm not going to tell her that, and she's neatening the place up, a bit ready for her family's return.

"I heard a man, a couple of doors down, disappeared, don't know if his house will be much help clue wise because his wife, Mrs Bell, is still there, she will have moved stuff by now."

"We could always question her, it's worth a try."

Making our way along the street, it is feeling empty. Most people on this street have disappeared or gone off to live with other members of family to protect each other. The abandoned feeling sends a shiver up my spine, all the unkempt gardens are a far cry away from the immaculately kept ones that we passed on the way here.

"It's this one here with the blue door."

I knock on the door, not sure if she will answer. Gertie told me she hadn't left her house and her curtains have been drawn since her husband went. I don't blame her.

"Who is it," there's a whisper through the door and slight movements.

"Hello, I am Adalyn."

"And it's Gertie, dear."

"Yes, and Gertie. We are just trying to piece stuff together, maybe you could help us."

"How can I help; I don't know where he is gone," she sounds enraged at my question.

"Please, it will be an immense help to us," I plead almost breathless from the need to find out more about what happened.

I hear more noises; it may be a key in the door. I nervously bite at my nails as we wait. Finally, the door opens not very wide but wide enough for me to see the woman on the other side. Her hair is all tangly and her skin dull, her eyes carry large bags. She gives us a quick look up and down and lets us in. We move fast because she starts to close the door before we even make it into the house. She hit the back of my foot and it hurt but I have no time to feel pain. I have a feeling she isn't going to want us to stay for long.

"What is it you want to ask," her words came out like they were a discomfort to her. We continue to stand, given the chairs are all full of mess, so is the floor.

"What was your husband doing before he disappeared? Were you with him?"

"No, if I was with him don't you think I would have stopped it from happening!" She runs her fingers through the front of her hair but leaves her palms covering her eyes.

"Yeah, sorry, bit of a stupid question there."

"A bit?" her tone is extremely sarcastic, more than mine usually is. "My husband is the best potion maker in this place, he is well desired. Before he vanished, he was trying to create a potion that gives you the best dreams you could wish for, moon drop potion he called it," she rolls her eyes. "I thought he should think about another name, he stripped off to his shed, didn't come back," she sighs.

"Naturally, I thought he'd got in such a huff he'd decided to stay with his mother. I didn't go around, I thought she would be loving it too much, us fighting. She never liked me, feeling is mutual. It wasn't till a few days later his mother came around complaining that she hadn't seen her son when I realised. I asked around for him, found out about others in the same situation, just no one thinking too much into it." We give her a moment to compose herself and grab a tissue. "No one runs away from here, why would they?"

"Is someone here?" I spot out of the corner of my eye something moving in the kitchen.

She follows my stare to the kitchen. "No, it's just my oon-oon; boo come here."

A little pink creature hops into the living room. Big blue eyes, the biggest I have ever seen, two small horns covered by its long sticking-up ears and it has hands. It's walking on two feet which resemble clown shoes and it may be the cutest thing I have ever seen.

"This is boo, she's my pet. She misses her daddy so much," she dabs her eyes with a tissue unable to carry on speaking.

"Hello, boo."

She turns around and hops back off into the kitchen, blanking my hello. It's not the first time an animal has ignored me, and I am sure it will not be the last. They seem to not like me even in another land.

"So he went to his shed. Is there any chance we could look in?" I go back into inspector mode.

"Knock yourselves out; I haven't been in properly myself, only to look if he was there."

She leads the way to the shed. It is much bigger than the one my dad owns, the one that holds all the half-finished projects that he got too angry at, to continue with. The walls are covered in shelves, all full of potions, so are the counters and in the middle is a big cauldron, a silver liquid still swirling around inside.

I take a look at some of the potions, 'tonic of health', 'a touch of forgiveness', 'elixir of joy', 'a tune of love', just to name a few but once again, no sign of struggle, not a single piece of glass laying on the floor that could have been knocked off during a squabble.

"Looks like he wasn't taken."

"I don't know, there's still a distance between here and the house; who's to say nothing happened between here and there."

I am channelling my inner curiosity, my keen eye for detail and my need to return home. I bend down to the grass, I accept the strange look I am getting from Gertie and Mrs Bell and search for clues. The pattern of the grass, was he dragged along, digging his feet in to the floor or if he has been taken, did the taker leave any evidence. One can hope.

"Why are you stroking the grass?"

"Why aren't you stroking the grass, this could be crucial evidence, you know." Gertie joins the search, patting the grass for no reason at all.

"I don't know what I am looking for?"

"For something, anything, a strand of hair, I don't know."

I get as close to the grass as possible, Mrs Bell leaves us to it, after giving a few distasteful looks, but doesn't disagree.

"I've found something," I lift a yellow diamond ring that was imbedded in the dirt. It looks expensive; I haven't seen one like it before. Gertie comes over to look, eyes wide at the finding.

"I'm not an expert but that looks real to me. Yellow diamonds are rare, never seen one before myself."

"Do you think it could be Mrs Bell's?"

"Bit of a weird thing to be laying around in your back garden, priceless they are."

"I think we should ask her."

We go back into the house, Mrs Bell in the living area just staring at the wall, tears filling her eyes, boo is mimicking her actions.

"Mrs Bell, I found this in your garden." I hand her a box of tissues I found on the kitchen side and sit down next to her amongst the rubble, holding the diamond ring on the palm of my hand.

She starts having a coughing fit when she catches sight of the diamond ring, peering in for a closer look. It also takes boo's interest, she starts taking swipes at the ring but is given a firm no from Mrs Bell and is now moping back in the kitchen.

"A yellow diamond! Wow, in my garden, where about?"

"It was in the dirt; I'll take that as it's not yours?"

"Definitely not, I wouldn't leave that in my garden for sure. The only person who ever had one of those was Maxim, the Queen's father, saw it on him when I met him one time. You do not think it's his, do you?"

I now have Gertie and Mrs Bell sat either side, giving the diamond admiring eyes.

"Wait, so this belonged to Maxim?" I close my hand around the diamond snapping them both back to reality.

"I haven't heard of anyone else who has had one. What is it doing in my garden? I swear I didn't know it was there, am I going to get in trouble?"

"I don't know how it got there and I doubt you will get in trouble; we need to go speak to the Queen."

I stand up, pulling Gertie with me and still clutching the diamond ring. “Thank you for your time, Mrs Bell, we are going to try our hardest to get your husband back.”

She smiles a half-smile like she wants to believe us but doesn’t know if she should, then shows us to the door.

Chapter Eleven

Gertie has been begging for a closer look of the ring but I daren't let go. It's not that I don't trust her, but she has an element of clumsy about her (not to mention the biscuit stained fingers) and in a few short moments, I will be sticking my arm down a drain trying to retrieve the diamond and I don't fancy getting covered in sewer. I do not even trust myself, seeing as clumsiness runs through my bones also. I am holding on to the ring like I am holding on to my life.

We pass the two gossipers on the way back to the castle, ogling at us like two ogling things. It takes them two seconds to realise who I am and that I am with Gertie and for them to turn to each other and have a good whisper, still keeping eye on us, so I wave at them just to be annoying.

"Hello ladies, been busy?"

"And what's that supposed to mean?"

"Your bags, you have a lot, had a busy day, shopping?"

"Oh, erm, yes."

"Well, I will see you later then, got a lot to do, you know, solving crimes and what not," I enjoy being smug. It's in my nature, always kill people with kindness, that's my motto.

Back at the castle and the guards let us in, no argument this time, and first time lucky getting in the prankster doors, I wonder if the door senses urgency. Winnie is out in the corridor, dusting the paintings on the wall.

"Hi, Winnie, do you know where the Queen is?"

"Oh, hi you two, she's out in the garden watering the plants."

"Thanks, Winnie."

Gertie's spotted a plate of biscuits in the living room and has decided she is peckish and wants one or ten biscuits. So I make my way along to the garden on my own, ready to show my finding to the Queen.

"Ah, Adalyn, I am just doing a spot of gardening. Don't the flowers look so alive, I do love this time of year, all the colour, it really lightens the mood," she pushes the fragrance upwards towards her nose, taking a drag of the fresh scent.

"My parents are keen gardeners. I've grew up knowing a lot about plants. I love the wide range you have."

"What is a garden without a few plants? Anyway, you must have come out here to tell me something." She looks down at my clenched fist.

"Have you found anything out?" I unscrunch my hand and reveal the diamond ring. Her eyes linger on the diamond but her facial expressions don't change. Once again, "My father's diamond; it vanished a long time ago, where did you find it?"

"It was in Mr and Mrs Bell's garden; Mr Bell went missing. I found it in the dirt. I was told about it being your father's. Mrs Bell didn't know how it got there, she was just as confused."

"I can imagine. It is a strange thing to find in your garden. May I?" She holds out a hand for me to put the diamond in. "My father never took this off his finger, when he," she stalls, "died, it went missing. It's a family heir loom passed on from King to Queen."

I think back to Winnie, telling me about Heston and killing Maxim.

"If you don't mind me saying, could Heston have taken it? Maybe he has returned?" She doesn't reply straight away, instead she looks at the Ceanothus tree in front of her.

"This is my favourite tree. If you see the trunk is curved, that's because my father moved it over here because he wanted it more in sight and the trunk started growing curved. That's why I like it, weird, I know... Yes, Heston took it and no, I don't think he has returned."

"Then, how can it have got here."

"Heston wouldn't return, for all I know, he may have died. He was power hungry, he wouldn't have hesitated to sell it, knowing its worth. He would not have held on to it. I was once close to him, I know; he wasn't one for family heirlooms. All he saw was how much things were worth, money wise," she gives me back the diamond. "I hope you do not linger on the perspective of Heston's return and that you look elsewhere for answers. I have faith you will find out what has happened." She takes a long deep breath, "What really happened?"

"Do you not want to hold on to your father's diamond?"

"You might need it, please hold on to it, keep it safe." She starts to walk away with her watering can in hand; I take that, as I should leave.

Gertie sat on the sofa holding on to her stomach, a plate that was once full, but is now empty, on her lap. Her face has a green tinge to it. I am staying well away.

"I don't feel too well."

“You don’t look too well either; how many biscuits have you ate?”

“I don’t know, I lost count after twenty.”

“How did you eat that many, I was gone like three-minutes max. We can’t work out our findings if you are going to vomit everywhere, at any given moment.”

“Just give me five minutes to nap and I will be right as rain.”

It takes her no time at all before she is passed out snoring away and I don’t even think ear-plugs will drown out the loudness. I want to throw a pillow at her, but she will probably wake up and be sick everywhere. Snoring sounds much more appealing. I hide the diamond in a trinket pot on the mantelpiece. It’s about time I do some shop exploring and given Gertie is out of it, and I am missing a partner, I have some spare time on my hands.

There is a door next to the kitchen door that I feel has been staring at me and calling me over. It has words engraved on it that say, ‘do not enter’ and the words have been tempting me to enter. I am telling myself, what’s going to be hiding in a room in the royal’s house that’s so bad that no one can enter. I was going to ask Winnie, but I thought about it and thought it would be best going to look myself because, like I said, what’s so bad? I have not heard any roars or any sort of noise to put me off exploring, where’s the harm?

I twist the golden handle with caution, while looking around, making sure the Queen or Winnie aren’t watching me from a distance waiting to pounce as soon as the door opens a crack. In the room, there is a long rustic table with matching chairs; pictures line the walls and a chandelier sits perfectly in the middle. It is a replica of the dining room we are actually allowed in, even down to the candle on the small table sat at the back. It's like something out of a scary movie, 'the evil doppelganger room'. Is something going to jump out and eat me. I can't understand why we wouldn't be allowed in or why they have copied and pasted a room.

"Adalyn, what's wrong?"

I almost knock the candle off the table but manage to stop it before it falls. Winnie stood staring at me by the door, holding folded towels.

"I know I shouldn't be in here. I was just curious; you know how it is, curious minds and all. Please don't tell Yvonne."

She looks confused; why is she confused? It is making me confused and now I can't get the word confused out of my head.

"Why wouldn't you be allowed in here, there's no time slot."

"But, it said 'do not enter', and I did."

She pulls a face like she just had a serious brain wave. "It's a prank door, put there by Oaky. You go in all excited, going through a door that tells you not to enter is fun, right, but then you end up confused and scared. It sends you in to a random room in the house. Believe me I tried it, so I know how you feel. You are lucky though, I ended up in the Queen's bedroom. I didn't recognise it; I was new, it was my first day and we aren't actually allowed in the Queen's room, she likes her own space. I went looking around, realised the Queen was fast asleep in bed. I panicked, knocked something over, woke her up and she screamed her head off, thought I was an intruder because we hadn't been introduced at that time. We don't speak about it now."

"I suppose it's only funny if you are in on the joke."

"Yep, I find people's reactions extremely funny now."

She walks off having a good old laugh to herself. Meanwhile, I forgot the candle was rocking on the edge of the table and gave it that extra push by accident so now I am glass-cleaning duty.

Back to the original plan of shop exploring and I am stuck at the doors once again. There's only so many times I can go through the prank door before I lose my mind and rip the door off the hinges. Sometimes, I feel like I have mastered picking the right door but I soon prove myself wrong.

"Did you get stuck at the doors again," the guards comment as I finally pick the right door.

"No, I didn't." I don't understand why they are laughing; since I have been here, they have made it through the door once on first try.

"Why is your face all flustered then?"

"Why is your face all flustered?"

"Eh."

"Exactly."

I push past them leaving them to ponder on that. I do really dislike them and they are the worst guards ever, they are constantly walking away from the gate; I feel like snitching on them to the Queen, wipe the smile straight off their faces. But I am not a snitch and can't be bothered to waste my breath on them. They clearly think their humour is wittier than it is. They remind me of someone…my dad.

I pass a shop that took my interest the other day, it has a baby blue shop front and highly decorated window displays. It reminds me of an adorable shop that pops up in every countryside village, so I decide to go in. They might sell little memorabilia. I could take them home to my family when I leave, they won't get it and will probably think I nicked it like they did the book; it may not be such a good idea. I shouldn't bring anything back, only for myself, not that I have any money. Maybe I should steal something, seeing as my parents think I do that any way.

It is very much unlike the countryside shops because I have never stumbled across one that sells bath bombs that actually do more than just fizz in your bath and then turn your water a different colour. One that is a shimmery pink ball says that if you put it in your bath, you will grow fairy wings for at least a minute and says, 'not suitable for fairies', that's got to be my favourite. Another is a bath bomb that is yellow, looks basic like the usual one you see in just about every shop but not the label. On this one, it says fills your room with sunshine, and that flowers will grow on top of the water. Interesting, I wonder how you bath with a bunch of flowers laying there. I read a few more; one will turn your bath water to lava, not something I see anyone wanting, although there does seem to be quite a few gone off the shelf. One that doesn't actually say what it does, only that it is a mystery. I wouldn't want to risk it. I don't like surprises and given that it's the deepest black and smells weird, nothing good is coming out of that one. The last one I read says it will make you be irresistible for twenty hours, maybe I should take that home for Carol, ha-ha. There are also scented candles that make you feel whatever they are named, so one here is calm and it says it will make you calm or there is an angry one that, like it says, will make you angry, etc...

I leave the shop and hear someone calling me, not by name but by, "oy, you ginger girl", that's kind, isn't it. I turn to see who is beckoning me in such a distasteful manner, to see a woman who sat in a small red tent that just about fits her and her table. She's placed in a corner, away from all the other shops and I don't think it's by choice. She tells me to come to her, which I really don't want to. It seems like it is a wrong thing to do, but I go anyway.

"Looks like you have been drawn here because you want to know your future," she is a fortune teller; I should have guessed, the crystal ball in front of her is a big give away.

"Actually, you told me to come here. I didn't even know you were there."

"It's okay to want to know your future, don't be ashamed, it is not frowned upon."

"Like I said, you called me here."

"Sit, sit, let me tell you what I see."

I sit; I really shouldn't because my mum told me that one time, she went to a fortune teller and it literally cost her a fortune. She was young and all her friends made her because they said she was amazing. The lady told her she will be married to a billionaire and she will meet this mystery rich man on the 22nd of March 1985, but that didn't happen and unless Dad is secretly rich and just denying me endless money, then I am one hundred percent certain on that.

The lady has her eyes closed, holding the crystal ball while breathing really heavily out of her nose, while I sit and think about how I can exit without her realising.

"Yes, I see it, I see it clear."

"What do you see?" I am taken in.

"I see it." If she could elaborate on that it would be fantastic.

"Oh, dear, yes, oh, that's not good, is it?"

"What's not good?"

She opens her eyes and holds out a hand. "That will be fifty baiters, please."

"You didn't even tell me anything and besides, I don't have any baiters."

"Not to worry, I am actually in need of an assistant."

"I am sorry, but you called me over here and did a really bad job at telling me my fortune."

"You have to pay your debt, somehow."

"I am surprised you didn't see in your crystal ball that I will not be paying for your services, or maybe you did."

She tries to argue but I make a swift exit before she can say another word. I am half expecting her to come running up behind, throw her crystal ball at me and knock me over like a bowling pin, but she doesn't.

The next shop along is a food shop and the one after that is a shop that sells the weirdest clothing I have ever seen. Now I understand why everyone's style of clothing is so wild, I got lucky with my flowery top and shorts.

"Hello, I've heard about your visit, I was hoping I'd bump into you." I turn and come face to face with a man; he is purple. A purple man. "I've heard you have been put on the disappearance case. Couldn't have come soon enough, my neighbour disappeared a few days ago, we were getting on like a house on fire." He winks. Ew, I actually cringe. "Are you on the right track to finding the missing?"

"I'm sorry about your friend but I can't say at the moment. It's too soon."

"Yes, I understand. If you need to know anything, please don't hesitate to ask."

"Thanks, I appreciate it."

He pats me on the shoulder and hands me a card with his address on.

"I'd love to see Birdie again. She is wonderful, you know, bakes the best lemon cake. I didn't think I'd find anyone being purple and all, it's hard for people to love a purple person, but she does, she told me but then, just like that, she was gone."

"Well, I'm proud of you, I hope you live a happy life together when she returns. I am actually in a hurry so can't stop, great talking, bye."

I walk away fast, back past the fortune-teller who luckily only catches sight of me when it's too late. I've decided to go back to the Queen's house. I feel somewhat out of place without Gertie. Maybe, by now she has come out of her food coma.

She is very much still asleep, snoring as loud as she was when I left. I heard her outside so that says a lot about how loud she is.

Night has fallen and I did not realise how starving I was until Winnie put a sandwich in front of me. I demolished it in seconds, and I am not ashamed to say.

Gertie wakes up with a jolt, scaring us all in the process, including herself.

"Where am I?"

"You are where you were when you stuffed all those biscuits in your mouth and passed out."

"Did I miss much?"

"Just a purple man telling me too much info about his neighbour."

"Ah, yes, Pointis will tell anyone with ears about his new lover. He must have told me a million and two times, sick a bit in my mouth every time."

There's silence in the room and I hear the hums once more from the still lanterns.

"What are the things in the sky, they come out at night."

"They are Illumers; they sleep in the light in the sleeping tree and at night they whisper their lullaby and produce light in the dark, if the Illumers go dark, it means we are no longer."

"They remind me of stars in a way."

"What are stars? I like that word."

"They sit in the night sky and shine, but they don't sing lullabies and as far as I am aware, they are really high up after all, but they definitely don't sleep in a sleeping tree."

We sit and just listen in silence, no speaking. It's the first time since being here that my head hasn't been full of questions. It's peaceful, that is until Gertie burps.

"Sorry, it's the biscuits. I'm not feeling good."

We burst out in spontaneous laughter; we are laughing that much, Gertie has tears down her face, and I am concerned about her lack of breathing and bright red face.

"I haven't laughed like that in a long time."

"Me either."

"I best be getting off. I feel all those biscuits making their way back up. I will be here bright and early, I don't expect you to be awake, but I am hoping to scam some breakfast out of Winnie, night."

"Night, Gertie."

I double check in the trinket box that the yellow diamond is still there and slip myself off to bed.

Chapter Twelve

Day three and another dream-less night. I fell asleep much easier last night; all the walking and investigating made me exhausted. So as soon as my head hit the pillow I was spark out. The nightgown has not grown on me and nor will it and I am in desperate need of a shower, one whiff of me and my smell would knock you clean out. You could also cook chips on my hair, the grease is that strong.

"Adalyn, I have some new clothes and food for you. Can I come in?"

"Yeah, sure."

Winnie walks in, a new outfit over her arm and a tray of toast and orange juice.

"Thought you would fancy toast today. I didn't know what flavour jam you liked so I put a mix in the pots."

"Thanks, is there any chance I could have a shower. I don't think anyone will want to come within miles of me the way I smell."

"Of course, it's just across the hallway. There are fresh towels on the rack."

"Thanks again, Winnie." She is always happy; she automatically puts you in an excellent mood, even if you don't want to be.

I cram my toast in my mouth and down the orange juice so I can get a quick start on the day. Today's outfit is a skater skirt and a basic top, I am happy with the simplicity of it. My shower is quick and cold, I didn't know how to adjust the temperature; it just has an on and off button, it took me twenty minutes to put just a toe under the water. I dry my hair in the bathroom mirror trying to smooth it straight, a far cry from its usual curly state. My pale complexion looks even more pale in the bathroom light; it makes my eyes look greener, sort of cat like.

I can hear Gertie talking downstairs; she is extremely loud and chirpy for this time in the morning. I do not know how she does it; I could easily sleep for another four hours.

"Hello, Adalyn, had a mare getting through the gates. Them stupid guards wouldn't let me in, they said I'm here too much and that the Queen hadn't even agreed to it and then I got stuck at the doors for half an hour. The guards were having a right laugh about it so I threw a stone at them. They said they were taking me to the dungeon, but Winnie came to my rescue again."

"They just enjoy winding people up. I wouldn't rise to it, as much as they do deserve a good rock to the face."

"Awful, the pair of them, no respect for their elders at all." She shakes her head in disappointment. "Before we get down to our investigations, I thought you might want to meet some of our creatures, especially the unicorns. I know how happy you were when you found out about them."

I have never wanted to do something so much in my life than to meet a real-life unicorn. "Of course, I want to."

"Let's go now then; I saw some unicorns out and about on my way here."

I can't even speak, I am that excited, my hands are shaking with happiness. When I was younger; I had a unicorn collection as big as my room. I would go as a unicorn for Halloween every year and not take the outfit off for about a month afterwards. The love never faded; I am, in fact, still unicorn mad.

We walk down the streets. I try and ignore the whispers, now that everyone knows who I am, I am a hot topic of conversation, thank you to the gossip Queens, not that I care. Gertie keeps telling me to not listen, that they are all just a bunch of gossiping idiots. It is the reason she doesn't like any one, she says, they aren't worth her time.

There is a group of children playing in the same place as before, showing each other their tricks and traits. One of them is using their mind to make the other children still like statues. I could stand and watch them all day, it's fascinating what they can do at such a young age and here I am…the only thing I can do is put my whole fist in my mouth and call it my party trick.

We reach the edge of a mini forest and Gertie stops. "Just a tip, don't touch the unicorns' face, they don't like it and if you come across a Tralebee, they are really fluffy, very adorable, don't go near. They trick you with their cuteness and then they open their mouths wide and eat you whole."

"What if it comes up to me without my permission?"

"They don't usually come up to you, but if they do, then run for your life."

"I don't want to go in now, I'm scared."

She slaps me on the back really hard; I wish she would stop doing that. I have said this before and I will say it again, she is strong.

“Give up, they won’t eat you, you’ll be fine.”

My back’s not fine; I am a hundred percent sure I am going to get a bruise.

“Right, don’t go shouting, you do talk rather loud, eh,” says she, “they will run away if you do.”

We creep into the forest. I can hear the creatures chowing down on their breakfasts and then scurrying away when we approach. I am hoping I don’t bump in to Tralebee although I am wondering how cute they actually are to lead you into such false pretences.

I feel a tap on my back, I grab on to Gerties arm, afraid at what may be lurking behind. Gertie turns around slowly and I see by her reaction that it isn’t a Tralebee and I am okay to turn around.

“She looks scared.”

There, in front of me, is a unicorn standing tall. I don’t feel in danger and this doesn’t feel real, a unicorn is right there and I am right here. Her aura feels magical and beyond anything, I can put into words. I stare at the unicorn’s perfectly swirled horn for longer than I should, her long red locks letting the only bit of wind whip through it. The sun peeking through the trees casts a sparkle in her eye. It is like I stepped into a fairy tale and come face to face with a creature that supposedly doesn’t exist, proving you shouldn’t always believe a nonbeliever.

“Let’s approach, slowly.”

At first, she takes two steps back as we get near, but Gertie reassures her we aren’t going to harm so she moves closer. I can see the rotting meat hanging out her mouth, but it doesn’t spoil her beauty.

“Remember, don’t touch her face, she won’t like it.”

I reach out a shaky hand and stroke her back, her hair is so soft, it's like it has been freshly conditioned. She rubs her head on my arm, closing her eyes as though she is drifting off to sleep.

A group of unicorns have come out from the trees to see what is going on but holding back a safe distance. They all have different coloured hair, one has ash brown, another has blonde with a little beard and the last but not least has brown; all are remarkable. They beckon her to join them which she does. And then they are off again, once more.

"They'll have gone off to play."

"You don't know how happy I am, Gertie. I'm constantly told Unicorns aren't real and there they were."

"Unicorns are one of the most powerful and clever creatures there is, and I suppose it's hard for people to admit their existence."

We start to make our way out the forest. I am one happy girl.

"What other creatures hang in this forest then; any more scary ones?"

"There's Goatchiecoots, they are big, and won't hesitate to kill whatever goes in sight, before you can even blink, you'll be dead. They are rare though, there's one way you can find out if one has been around."

"How?"

My mum always tells me to look where I am going but I don't listen. I never look at what's in front of me. I always look elsewhere because I know best. Today is the day I realised that I do not know best and maybe, just maybe, my mum is always right. I am currently face down in poo.

"Goatchiecoots always leave the biggest poo behind, apparently it's good for the skin," she says this while covering her nose and handing me the smallest bit of tissue, which I accept. I do not appreciate her laughing though.

"I'm going back to the house to have the longest shower ever, cold shower or not, and please, Gertie, don't laugh because I will come up to you and I will hug you and share this delightfulness with you."

"You wouldn't."

"Watch me."

I head towards Gertie, arms outstretched until there's a noise, somewhere behind Gertie. We both freeze. It is like someone is chomping their food through a megaphone.

"Gertie, what do we do?" I am covered in poo and may get eaten any second. How can the best day ever turn in to the worst day in seconds.

"It might be a Goatchiecoot, we need to stay still."

"If we stay still, we are going to get eaten, Gertie."

"And if we move, we are going to get eaten."

"It can't eat us if we are running."

"It probably just wants to know why you have been laying in its poo," she is laughing at her own joke silently and resembles a tomato.

"I'm going, I am not standing here like this all day, not a chance."

I start running, which makes Gertie run, why she has to scream when running I'm not sure, but she was the one who just a second ago, was making a big deal about moving.

We are out of the forest and into safety. Everyone moves out the way once they realise what I am covered in; a lot of people are telling me that I stink and have something on my face, like I do not know, like the smell isn't making me gag and I just happen to be covered in animal faeces without knowing.

Gertie barges past the guards and gets through the doors quick. She has not stopped running since the forest. I did, because it makes the poo more uncomfortable. I do not need to barge past any one because they voluntarily move. I thought I smelt bad this morning, but it was nothing compared to now.

I got through the doors straight away. Maybe it sensed my anger or even they think I reek bad. I do not go searching for Gertie, I go straight to the shower.

"Hi, Winnie, could I have a change of clothes, if possible."

She doesn't ask questions, but she looks confused. "Sure I'll put them on your bed." She is practically running away; I don't blame her.

I scrubbed myself, I have used a full bottle of body wash and shampoo. I didn't even care about the cold. The unpleasantness will not leave me, it's just lingering.

I am not bothering with my hair this time. It is going to have to be wild because who knows when I am going to fall in another pile of poo and must wash my hair once again.

I go down in my fresh new outfit and can hear Gertie having a good old giggle on my behalf.

"Having fun."

Winnie is also there, wiping away her laughter tears.

"I'm glad to see the poo off your face, I wasn't lying when I said it's good for the skin," that sets her and Winnie off again. "You should have seen her, Winnie, face down hilarious."

"Thanks, Gertie, don't you think we should get back to the task in hand instead of laughing at my misfortune."

"You're right, but it is funny, Adalyn. I'll be laughing at this for years to come." Brilliant.

"What's the plan then, Adalyn?"

"I need to find out if Heston did sell the diamond. The Queen said she thinks he did, and that there's no way he has anything to do with the disappearances, but I think otherwise."

Gertie's face turns pale, her smile gone. "You think Heston has returned?"

I look around checking if Winnie is out the room. "Shh, Gertie, I don't know. I can't say I am certain but it's weird, isn't it? Maxim had the yellow diamond, then it disappeared when he died. The only person that could have took it is Heston and everyone knows the diamond belonged to Maxim; they wouldn't buy it from a murderer who stole it," saying it out loud really makes me believe my theory.

"But someone would have seen Heston. Anyone being odd around here won't get away with whatever they are doing."

"I know, I've not worked that bit out yet."

"What's next on the list then, more evidence taking or more interviews?"

"We need to ask around about the yellow diamond. Are there any shops that buy used things and then sell them on?"

"Not a shop but there is a person, Walter Eldred, and I know where he lives."

"Lead the way, Gertie, I think we need to speak to this man."

Chapter Thirteen

We reach a house that is not easy on the eye like the others. In fact, there is a big hole in the roof, a metal can on fire on the front garden and chunks of missing grass. I am afraid to go through the gate that is hanging off its hinges, because once my feet are at the other side, who knows what I am going to stand on. I'll have to play a game of dodge the unknown object. If he had that diamond and sold it, surely he would not be living in this questionable looking house.

There's a smell lingering outside the house. I don't even know what the smell is, it's like a mixture of the smoke from the lit can, body odour and onions. It is worse than how I just smelt not so very long ago, and that was bad. If the smell carries on into the inside, I am not going to be able to stay there for long, without being sick.

"This doesn't look like a clever idea." Gertie is twiddling her fingers with an anxious look on her face.

"It doesn't smell like one, either."

Before I even get to knock on the door, it swings open and a man wearing a dirty tank top and shorts stood where the door once was. My hand is still in knocking hold and there's terror in my eyes, also tears, because of the smell.

"What do you want?"

"I was just wondering."

"Well, go wonder somewhere else," he goes to shut the door, but I stick my foot in before he can. "What are you playing at."

"I was just wondering if you know anything about the yellow diamond."

He looks offended and even angrier than before, if that's possible. "You think I've stole it. I've heard this all before from the Queen's mother, wondering if I had the stupid yellow diamond. Well, I haven't. I never have. I'm not interested in that yellow diamond, it doesn't tempt me. Shiny things don't tempt me," he's waving a hammer around as he talks. I've had to duck several times. "Even when Maxim came to find out its worth," he spits on the floor next to my foot and rubs his shoe in it, "but even if I did have it, why would I tell you and old Gertie over there," he slams the door shut before I can reply, wafting the stench into my face. Sick, literally came up my throat.

"Who's he calling old, he looks way older than me."

"Gertie, we don't have time to be annoyed about who called whom what. He didn't have the diamond so he must not have sold it. Do you know anyone else who sells things?"

"Nah, he's the only one dodgy enough to have a diamond, knowing it belonged to the king."

"What if he's lying? Like he said, he wouldn't tell us?"

"He won't have it, to be honest. I don't think he would be able to afford it in the first place. Heston would not sell it for naught," fair point she made.

"We need to think of something to do next, away from here, the stench is stinging my nose."

“Clear off.” The man is sticking his head out the window throwing bits of food at us. No wonder his house stinks.

“We were, you grumpy git.” Gertie picks up one of the thrown items of food and throws it back, hitting him square in the face. His eyebrows narrow even more as he wipes away the debris from his face. Next second, we are legging it down the road, away from Walton’s clenched fists.

“I’ll get you, Gertie.”

We have ducked behind a wall, both absolutely exhausted. Gertie doesn’t half-put us in some situations.

“Why do you think Maxim went to find out its worth?”

“Would I be wearing that treasure, I’d need to know how much,” she rubs her thumb against her index finger and middle finger, “I am wearing on my finger.”

“I suppose.” I don’t think I’d want to know how much it is worth; I’d be a nervous wreck every time I put it on.

A lot more people are being polite to me as we walk down the street in the beaming sun, back to the house, with no latest information. I’ve gotten hellos from every direction, even from the gossiping ladies from the other day.

“Some flowers, to brighten up your day.”

A lady at a flower cart hands me a bunch of daisies, as we pass, with a little greeting card on. It reads ‘thank you for coming to our rescue’, very sweet. Gertie is standing in front of the lady for her bunch of flowers, but I don’t think they are coming; the lady is just looking at her like something she stood in.

“Here, you can have mine.” I have not seen Gertie’s smile so big before and she is constantly smiling. I slip the greeting card in my pocket though; I don’t want Gertie to think she’s not being appreciated for her help as well.

"I love daisies, my favourite flower," she says, as she inhales the scent for the billionth time. I bet it is a blessing to her nostrils, complete opposite to what they have just had to go through at Walton's house.

We get back to the house and the guards let us straight in, without bothering us. They look way too warm sitting under the sun to be annoying, sweat is dripping down their face, empty water bottles surround them and ice packs rest on their legs.

The house looks like it has gone through a thorough cleaning; I can see my face in the floor. That isn't even an exaggeration either. I just saw that I had toast stuck in my teeth and no one told me.

"Hey, you two, did you enjoy seeing the unicorns?" she chuckles, remembering my misfortune earlier. Winnie sat at the dining room table having her dinner. To me, it looks really unappetising, but she seems to be really enjoying it. I try and get the food out of my teeth with my tongue before replying. I am blocking out her little giggles.

"Yep, best day ever, sort of," I say through closed lips, it's harder than you think.

"I love the unicorns; I go down and feed them. They love apples, the really red ones and raw meat. I never forget the raw meat; it's their favourite." That explains a lot.

"Winnie, do you know much about the yellow diamond?"

"I know that it belonged to the Queen's father and it was taken on his death bed. Not many people know this. It's not something that is out there, so you can't go spreading it around." Her eyes flicker towards Gertie. "The diamond isn't just a diamond, it's Oaky's own power concealed into a diamond. When he was dying, he didn't want his powers to go to waste. He was the most powerful wizard there ever was. He didn't want that to die with him, so he found a way to conceal it so it could be given to someone who really needs it."

I get the ring out the trinket pot and put it on the table in front of Winnie. Her mouth opens from the shock. This reaction looks awfully familiar. "So you're telling me, this isn't just a diamond?"

"Yes, where did you find it? It's being missing for so long."

"We found it in the garden of one of the people who went missing."

"How did it get there?" Is she talking to me or the diamond?

"We don't know, but it's got to have something to do with it. I have a feeling Heston is the reason for the disappearances"

She finally looks at me and not the diamond. "Heston's returned?"

There's a cough from by the door, causing the room to go silent.

"Sorry to disturb, I thought it would be a good idea for you all to join me for a meal tonight. I realised I hadn't spent the time getting to know you, Adalyn, maybe it is time to do so and you can update me on your findings."

How did she manage to sneak through the door unheard. I hope she didn't hear any of that conversation. I am silently panicking; my heart is beating fast. She told me to put my assumptions about Heston to bed, but instead she has caught me telling Winnie. I wonder if the dungeons are comfortable.

The doors open and a head pops around. It's one of the guards from outside. This may be the first time I am happy to see one of the guards. He is my saviour and I thank him dearly.

"There's a woman outside asking for you, Adalyn. She said her name is Mrs Bell." I rise to my feet.

"Let her in," Yvonne says, "remember our meal please, 7 pm." She leaves the room without a second look.

Mrs Bell's timing is impeccable. I don't know what she is coming to say, but the fact she has left her house for the first time since her husband disappeared, makes me think it's important.

"Hello, Adalyn, I'm sorry for coming without informing you, but a man came earlier asking if he can come in my house. I said no and he wasn't happy about it. His face was covered, unfortunately, I couldn't see what he looked like. I had to grab a neighbour to watch my house, so I can let you know; I came as soon as I could."

"Show me which way he went."

I scoop the ring up, then me and Gertie follow Mrs Bell down the streets. I've got stich from walking so fast, also a banging stress headache from not knowing how much Yvonne heard. Everyone is staring at us; I don't know if it's because we are walk-running, or if it's because Mrs Bell has left her house. Either way, they can stare away.

"He went this way," she points down the long empty street. I try and work out how long it will take someone to escape and hide.

"I'm going to go and look."

"Don't be stupid, Adalyn, you could get hurt."

I ignore Gertie's words and take off running down the street, hoping I don't find the only stone on the path and trip.

The stich is now unbearable. I clutch my chest in agony but carry on running, looking up the paths to the houses in case he is hiding. I fell for one or two shadowy figures that just turned out to be nothing, which has put me back a few seconds.

I see the end of the street approaching and so far, no Heston (who I only presume is the hooded figure) or legitimate dark shadows up a path. I hit the edge of another mini forest and dare myself to go in. I stand there in front of the trees listening to the scurrying and rattling, looking in to the unknown now; the sun isn't bright enough to cast light in to the pit of darkness. Daring myself didn't work and the calls of Gertie and the begging of my stich make me retreat back.

I take my time returning, checking behind me every two seconds, hoping but also not hoping that I see Heston behind me. I hadn't planned out what I would do if I come face to face with him. I don't think my sarcasm and talent for giving painful nips will quite cut it. I think he may be a wizard as well; he'll just laugh in my face if I try go up against him on my own. Not a single bit of power or knowhow about how to use the ring, I will be dead within seconds.

Gertie is shaking her head at me as I approach, arms crossed as well. She reminds me of my mum and Dad when I take late night walks and don't tell them. I stroll through the door and they are stood there, exactly how Gertie is now except they ground me, and Gertie doesn't have that sort of responsibly over me to do that.

"Don't do that again, Adalyn, you could have got hurt. You are lucky he wasn't there."

"I didn't want him to be right there and slip through my fingers."

"You can't go risking your life like that. Mrs Bell said she's putting a pot of tea on and I am parched, come on." Sitting down sounds more appealing at this moment in time, my head is ringing.

"I hope Gertie has given you a telling-off because if she hasn't, I'm going to," Mrs Bell is waving a cup around in time with her words. Her hair is much less wild than the last time I saw her.

"She has."

"Good. I can't believe you went after someone that may be part of these disappearances, you risked a lot there," looks like I am getting another grilling then, "did your parents not teach you to not go after strangers."

"It is more like not talk to strangers than follow them. I think its common sense not to follow them."

"And you didn't use any common sense, did you? Does anyone take sugar in their tea."

"No," we both reply in unison.

"If I knew you would try go after him, I wouldn't have told you which way he went."

"We need to know how all the people disappeared and if that means going after strange characters, I'm going to have to, with or without your permission."

She hands me a piping hot cup of tea and puts a plate of biscuits on the table. Gertie's eyes light up, then I see her holding her stomach and she pushes the plate away. Last night's feast must have put her off, which doesn't surprise me. I felt sick at the thought of how much she ate.

"No biscuits for you, Gertie?"

"No thanks, not hungry."

I take a couple and dunk them in my tea. I hope the tea doesn't taste like how the Queen's did because there's nowhere to pour this one without Mrs Bell seeing.

"I remembered something yesterday after you left. I am not sure how relevant this is, but my husband told me the day before he disappeared that someone had asked for a whole bunch of potions making. He turned it down because he thought it was weird, them asking for the things they did. Stupidly, I didn't ask what they wanted because at the time I thought nothing of it. It still might be nothing, but everything helps, eh."

I take my first sip of tea and ponder on her words; I am relieved that it tastes like proper tea and that I don't have to make an excuse as to why I won't be drinking it. Gertie is staring at the biscuits. I don't think she heard a word Mrs Bell just said, she is under biscuit hypnotism.

"Do you know anything more, like where he was when he asked him or just anything?"

"Sorry, no, like I said I didn't think to ask. Ridiculous, I know, but when he was telling me about it, I was miffed at him for not hanging the washing out, so wasn't really wanting to speak with him. It sounds ridiculous now, arguing about a stupid washing pile. Now, he's not here."

It seems weird that I am inside a book that is full of magic and things that no one will ever believe if I told them in my world, and yet they still have arguments about hanging the washing out.

"It's fine, you have been a big help."

At this moment Boo, the oon-oon, appears, spots me and Gertie and runs off hiding behind the curtains, she doesn't know though that the curtains are transparent, we are staring straight at her.

"Boo what are you doing, they are your friends. Boo gets very scared a round new people."

Boo is not paying attention and still stood there behind the curtain making weird noises that sound like she is saying, 'wow', repeatedly.

"You mind if I go settle her, it's her nap time. I'll be back down in a sec."

She picks up a nervous Boo and exits the room. It has taken Gertie mere seconds to scoff the remaining biscuits, I knew she would.

The Illumers are out; they really make you feel like you aren't alone. The last remaining shoppers hoping to grab a bargain, are now making their way home. The closed signs have all made their appearances on the shop doors and the street sweepers are out, cleaning for a new day that approaches. I pass them and bid them good night, they wish me a good night and get back to their duties.

The daytime guards have been replaced with the night-time guards, the friendly ones that don't have a laugh at your expense when you can't get through the doors.

"Hello, Adalyn, you look tired."

"I'm exhausted. Night, you two."

Two struggles later and I get through the doors. I decide not to go into the living room but instead head upstairs, to neaten myself up for the awkward dinner that is approaching. Gertie went home to, and I quote, "put on her best dress". Meanwhile, I just neaten my hair with my fingers and stick it in a bobble.

I prepare myself for the uncomfortable meal, patting at the bumps in my bobble like it will magically tame it. My mind is drifting between thoughts of my family and the happenings in this land. I can't seem to focus on just one.

"The Queen asked me to come get you, I just got here myself." Gertie is standing beside the door. I didn't expect a knock and a 'can I come in', seeing as I don't get one at home.

I follow Gertie downstairs to the dining room. Yvonne's sat at the end of the table, she doesn't speak, just nods. I copy but she looks away just as I did, so for my own sanity and because I am too much of an awkward person, I change it to looking around the room very dramatically like I have never been in this room before, then take my seat.

"I thought a meal together will help us get to know each other better." Winnie places a bowl of soup in front of us all including herself then sits across from myself.

"Tell us about yourself, Adalyn. I don't know a thing about you."

I sip my soup and begin to speak.

"Well, I am an only child. I have a weekend job at a garden centre, which I hate; it is the staff I hate. I don't have any friends as I am home schooled, and I don't know any one my age. Although my parents' friends' children think I am their friend, I do not think so. Their idea of fun is tiggy bob down and they think my face is their drawing canvas. The place I live is boring so I just spend my time window shopping and sleeping." Did I breathe during my reply, I can't remember.

"What is this tiggy bob down?" Yvonne asks with genuine curiosity.

"It's a game children play, when jumping in human sized bubbles isn't possible."

She looks surprised.

"What sort of things do the children like to draw then?" She's not very good at asking normal questions.

"It's mainly squiggly lines and glasses. But a lot of the time it's things they learnt in the school playground, from that one child that knows all the rude stuff," Yvonne is nodding along but I know she doesn't have a clue what I am on about.

"Interesting, so Gertie and Adalyn, how is the investigation going?"

"It's going," I reply.

"To me, it seems someone has gone rogue. It's the only explanation."

"Oh, I didn't know it is the only explanation. Please enlighten me to how the ring just magically appeared after all these years in someone's garden, because I am struggling to find a logical explanation and you seem to have all the answers."

Her lips are pursed. "As you must know things happen without explanation, it could have been there for some time now. Who's to say it didn't get caught on to Mr or Mrs Bell's self by mistake and brought on to the garden."

I bite my tongue to stop the words I have brewing. It's like her eyes are closed from the truth and she is trying to make anything else seem legit. Gertie's slurps of her soup sound much louder than before. I am just trying to drown out the noise Yvonne is making and Gertie's slurps sound much more interesting.

"I just wouldn't think too much about the ring. It will put you off topic."

I stand up ignoring her last comment, "If you don't mind, this conversation has put a sour taste in my mouth and I am tired. This meal is just very inconvenient, so I'll pass on the soup. Night Gertie, Winnie, Yvonne, see you all tomorrow. Maybe we will all be talking sense."

The fairies are out and about in the hallway, giggling away, clearly up to something, but I'm not going to bother asking because I am too wound up.

"We heard you arguing," the blue fairy comments and the giggling starts again.

"Good for you." I carry on walking away.

"Is it about that ring, the one that was her family's?"

There's clearly something funny about it that I don't know about.

"The old aide had it when Maxim died. We took it from her and hid it in our house. It was funny, but we had to give it back because Maxim got angry and threatened to knock our houses down." I stop at the end of the stairs.

"But you just said he died; how did he get angry?"

They both shrug and blow fairy dust in my face, right in my eye. Now they have zoomed off laughing their heads off and set off a flower explosion; Yvonne won't be happy and quite frankly that makes me happy. They must be confused with Heston because I can't make any sense from what they just said. Why did the aide have the ring though, that bit doesn't make sense. I'm not even sure if I should believe a word they say, they like a joke at other people's expense; they'll have heard us speaking and concocted a story.

I put on my new pyjamas, a plain tee and plain trousers Winnie has left for me. I am so angry, beyond angry. Why get me here if she's not going to care what I have to say and come up with her own scenarios, which are wrong. I am following my own leads, whether she likes it or not. And as for what the fairies have said, I'm ignoring them.

My eyes start to feel heavy, I let the hums of the Illumers carry me to sleep.

Chapter Fourteen

Day four; I am as tired if not more than before I went to sleep and as much as I lay there with my eyes closed pretending to my brain that I am asleep, I can't physically go back to sleep.

I don't hear Gertie's loud talking which tells me she isn't here; it doesn't surprise me. In the night, Winnie and Gertie woke me up, so I went to go tell them to shh, only to see Gertie stood there, a bottle of wine in one hand and a glass in the other. She was just drinking straight out the bottle, there was no reason for the glass, then a guard came in and escorted her home. As for Winnie, she started crying then passed out on the sofa. So I do not expect to see them for a long time, they were very drunk.

I get dressed and make my way downstairs; on the day I wish I had a tray of breakfast in front of me so I can just sit in bed and eat it, Winnie is not here and is more than likely cooped up in bed, with a sore head. So it's no breakfast in bed and instead I am off to raid the cupboards.

So food options are as listed:

Porridge

Toast

Something that looks like yogurt but with a layer of mould in it.

Or a tin of peaches.

Tin of peaches it is. I haven't a clue how to make the toast, there is no toaster. How does Winnie make it?

I'm in the middle of eating my peaches when the Queen walks in. I automatically hide the peaches behind my back, like I have done something wrong, you know when you have that feeling you shouldn't be eating something because it may be for someone else, that's the feeling I have.

"Good morning, Adalyn, how was your sleep?" She opens the cupboard door and seems to be looking for something. I hope it's not the peaches.

"It was alright, thanks." I'm not apologising for yesterday, but do I mention what happened. She is all smiley and it's weird I thought she would be in a mood.

"That's good."

She moves on to the next cupboard, I am feeling all panicky. What if I have her peaches, that and the whole Heston thing may just get me thrown in the dungeon.

"You looking for anything in particular."

"Just my peaches. I must have ran out."

I hold onto the peaches tight behind my back.

"Maybe, would you like me to pick you some up?"

"No, it's fine. I've asked too much of you already. I will ask one of the guards to. Winnie isn't very well today, I gave her the day off."

I give her my best nonsuspicious smile and sidestep away, in a fashion where she can't see the tin of peaches I am hiding. Now, I am out of sight, I make a break for it outside to finish the rest of the peaches. I am going to find Gertie. Yesterday felt like a waste, minus the unicorns, and I need Gertie by my side to finally crack the case.

The streets are quite bare, given the time, most shops aren't open yet, there's just one or two loiterers. I don't know whether I remember where Gertie lives. She pointed to it the other day, but the houses on her street all looked the same.

"Hi, Adalyn." A young girl has stopped in front of me, she has a dark sapphire crystal in her forehead which matches her eyes down to a tee. She's all smiley and waving.

"Hello, erm, I don't know you name." I try so hard not to look at the crystal, but it's hard not to. It's remarkable.

"My name is Vienna; my crystal is a symbol of my knowledge, if you were wondering."

I quickly divert my eyes, "I'm sorry, I wasn't being rude."

"It's ok, I like my crystal. It's pretty and shiny, even though other children say it looks freaky."

"It's not freaky and you should like it, don't let anyone tell you otherwise. I like it. I think it suits you." She looks so happy; it makes me happy. "Are you out on your own?" She must be about six or seven-year-old.

"Yes, just picking up some bread," my parents would have never let me go pick up bread at her age. They still don't trust me now when I'm out and about on my own.

"Do your mum and Dad know?" she looks at me really perplexed as if I asked if she is spinning on her head.

"Of course, they do."

"Right, well, I best be going, Vienna. I will see you another time. Remember not to listen to anyone when they are mean. Stay safe."

"I will, Adalyn, c'ya soon."

She skips merrily away and I'm still none the wiser about why our encounter just happened. I thought she was going to ask me something, I do feel I learnt a lesson from her though.

As I flounder up the naked streets, my mind lost in space, considering asking to go home now. I catch sight of someone in a hooded cape, like Mrs Bell described, face-covered. I stop and watch with suspicion; he catches sight of me, and we enter a staring competition. My eyes are taking in his every move, I can see I am making him nervous, his hands twitching. Why isn't he running and why am I am not running towards him, tackling him to the floor.

A lady, pulling a stroppy kid behind her, blocks my view. He takes his chance to get away but it's not going to happen today. I run like I have never run before, catching up to him fast by jumping over all the objects that block my path. He's gaining speed but I am gaining more. I throw my body out tackling him, grabbing his arm, and pulling it behind his back.

"Where is everyone, Heston? What have you done with them."

"I don't know what you are on about, get off me."

"You think I believe what you say."

I rip his hood off his head. There in front of me is the face of Maxim Tolstem, the man that was supposedly murdered by his cousin, there, staring up at me. My grip untightens and he almost slips away.

"But, you're dead."

"Clearly."

"It's been you, all along."

"Do you think I am going to explain myself to some child? Wait, you're that one they brought in to save the day, the big shot. So the rumours are true; you look like you can't even fasten your shoelace yet, never mind save the day."

"Big words for someone who's just been tackled to the floor by the girl that can't fasten her own shoelace yet. Do you know your daughter is in despair over all this? Do you know what you have done to her! She was right, it wasn't Heston."

"She will understand in the end why I have done all this, but for now, ba bye." he's set off running again down the street, I try to catch up to him but I struggle; he's too fast this time.

Chapter Fifteen

So, I have reached a house that I think is Gertie's. It's got Gertie written all over it, not literally but the garden is full of ornaments, crazy like herself. I knock as loud and clear as possible. I ran past everyone like a mad lady on the way here, accidently pushing everyone out the way. My red face and grouchy attitude must have looked charming.

"Gertie, answer. I need to tell you something. It's important, please answer." I bang louder. "Gertie." I look through the windows. I don't hear or see her which is concerning.

"Gertie, you in there?" No reply.

"Gertie, it's Adalyn. Please answer, it's important."

"Gertie, isn't home." There's a man sweeping his path next door.

"How do you know?"

"She's set a ridiculously loud alarm that goes off every time she opens the door. I haven't heard it since yesterday around six thirty when she was leaving her house."

"Maybe it's broke."

"Believe me; Gertie won't let her alarm break."

"Oh, well, thanks. If you see her, will you let her know I am looking for her?"

"Yes." He carries on sweeping leaving me well and truly baffled. Maxim's taken her.

I get back to the house and the Queen sat in the living area. I have something to tell her and I am afraid to do so. If she didn't believe Heston is behind it, she's not going to believe what I have to say.

"Hi, have you seen Gertie?"

"I haven't, sorry, is she missing?"

"She went home last night. She was drunk but a guard took her back. Her neighbour said she's not home and not been home since six thirty yesterday."

"Have you checked in the shops?"

"I had a look through the windows on the way here, I hung around for a little bit outside them just in case, but she wasn't there."

"Do you think Gertie could have been taken? Maybe she has stayed somewhere else."

"I need to tell you something. You aren't going to like it or believe it, but it's not Heston behind the disappearances, it's Maxim."

She dabs away the tea drop off her chin. "My father is dead; I don't appreciate you coming into my house, slating my father's name. He was a good man."

"I don't want to be the one to tell you this, but he isn't. He is well and truly alive and he is the reason for all these disappearances. I need you to believe me, I saw him, I tackled him to the floor and spoke to him, he was there."

"I do not believe lies; I don't know what you're playing at, Adalyn, but it seems Mrs Read had the wrong end of the stick when she picked you. I'm sorry but I want you to go."

"I am not going anywhere; my friend has gone, nearly everyone's family has gone and you are going to sit there and ignore facts. I saw him and if you don't want to believe it then that's your choice but as Queen, I thought you would be doing a bit more than sitting around drinking tea and being in denial. I am not bothered about you calling me a liar, what I am bothered about is you not taking in what I am saying because you don't want your father to have a bad name. Well, it's too late for that. Now, if you don't mind, I am going to go figure this one out on my own, as I don't have Gertie anymore and it seems I don't have you either." I leave the room slamming the door behind me, my whole body is shaking with anger.

"Wait." I turn and see the Queen standing at the door, tears in her eyes.

"I believe you and I want to help. Give me a second to change out of this dress and change into something suitable for our tasks ahead."

I can't deny, I didn't think that was going to happen. I thought she might start to believe me, but I didn't think she would offer to help.

I sit and wait for what feels like forever. I hope she's not changing into a ball gown. Not only will her, in a ball gown, make me look much more of a mess, her all glammed up to the max, but she will be very over-dressed for the situation.

She returns with joggers on and a vest top; who knew the Queen owned joggers. They resemble the pair my dad owns, plain grey. He bought them because he saw a young man wearing them so they must be in fashion; his words, certainly not mine. I begged him not to wear them in public or in the house, he doesn't listen. Even Mum has told him to put them at the back of the wardrobe and leave them there.

"Right, what are we waiting for, let's go find these people then."

I can see by the redness round her eyes that the reason she was so long is because she was crying, I don't blame her.

"I should have told you from the beginning how to know which door is not the prank door. The door handle never changes, if you look, this door handle has markings on, that is for the proper door, the plain handle is the prank door, all the time."

So given the guards don't know that, that means the Queen likes a good prank also. So, her straight face and moody act is a mask, or she just doesn't like the day guards as well, like the rest of us.

"Hello, mam, can we help you with anything?" They look her outfit up and down.

"Not today, just guard the house. I can't say when I will be back; I don't need a guard," she says to the now standing guard. "Thank you though, the house is the only thing that will need guarding."

"So, what's the plan?" I ask, as we move out of earshot from the guards.

"There's a place my dad loved to go, it's quite a distance so I hope you got your walking shoes on," she looks at my shoes, not walking ideal, "or at least some comfortable ones." They aren't comfortable either.

Yvonne hasn't thought to disguise herself. Many people are popping out the shops to say hi and have a glimpse at her majesty wearing her joggers, there's plenty of pointing at her legs, not even they can disguise her. We have some curtain twitches that would prefer to sneak looks and gossip later than to approach. Yvonne politely tells everyone who comes up to speak, to back off (ok, she doesn't say back off, but she may as well), that she is on duty and has no time to speak. They mostly all respect what she has to say, except some that just presume she isn't speaking to them, they join in telling everyone to leave the Queen alone but won't go themselves; that's until Yvonne says, "I mean everyone", and they strut away like they don't care who she is any way.

We get to the edge of the forest where my nerves got the better of me and wouldn't let me stumble in to the unknown.

"Follow me and stay close."

I follow her orders, staying close as we take the first steps in. Yvonne doesn't seem to be bothered that a bear could pop out and eat us whole (that's if they have them here). I know her mind is not in the forest, it is elsewhere. I wouldn't blame her if she just stopped and screamed the trees down.

I have tripped over many sticks and stones, lost my shoe on numerous occasions and almost made the Queen deaf; I squealed in her ear because a bird flew past and frightened the day lights out of me. She didn't appreciate that one.

This forest wouldn't look so scary if more sun light was able to make its way through the trees. I wouldn't have tripped so much either. The last thing I thought about bringing was a torch and that's the first thing I need. The dark shadows cast by the trees and other mysterious objects give me the heebie-jeebies, so much so that I find myself clutching on to Yvonne's arm without realising and then being shunned by her.

There's no clear path either, complete opposite to the welcoming forest I came through when I first got here. I suppose the forest that holds the unicorns wasn't that much of an improvement, but the trees were further apart so light wasn't an issue. It didn't have the creepy factor, it was way more magical.

"We aren't far away, it's just through these trees."

We step through a tree archway that has led us to a circle of grass, no trees, and a fountain in the middle with benches around it. It looks like it once had a certain charm to it and a go to place but now it looks lost and forgotten.

She goes up to a tree, the odd tree out, so to say, one that it bright and not wary, with engravings on that reads 'Maxim + Mae'. She takes the tip of her finger, not paying attention to her parents' names and runs it down the tree and as by magic a door appears, one that is like the door in the tree I first came through. She opens the door and goes in, not waiting for me to enter first or letting me know what's going on. I step through and what I see is not an attractive sight. The grass has dried, the sky is dull, the air isn't fresh, and it feels cold, really, really cold. The beauty and the colour has not carried on through this door. It's like how I imagine stepping through a parallel universe feels like. I can see a house nothing special about it, very run down and no bubble gum scented smoke coming from the chimney, but a grey cloud casting a dark shadow over an already dull house.

"We should go to the house."

"I think you should go back," her words rolled out like they were waiting on the tip on her tongue for the right moment.

"What, no I'm not going back, are you joking?" I don't take her words seriously; after all, she is the one that practically begged me to stay and help when I first arrived here, she can't back track at such a crucial part.

"I am not joking, this could be dangerous. I can't put you through that, I know my father's skills."

"I am not bothered, I am putting myself through it. Do you think I will just agree and take myself back to the house and make myself a pot of tea, pretend nothing's going on!"

"I shouldn't put this sort of pressure on you, especially at such a young age."

"Well, it's a bit too late for that one."

"Fine, but you follow me." She reluctantly agrees to me staying.

Now that I know she would much rather go this alone, it makes me want to show my strengths even more so than before, maybe I needed that push. I hold my head high, puffing out my chest to make myself seem confident and don't have a nervous stomach pain currently sitting on my bladder.

As we get closer to the house, I spy behind it a barn, run down also but with a little renovating, I am sure it will make a lovely home; I have seen people do it on the TV.

We step through the front door and the atmosphere is tense. Yvonne is familiar with her surroundings, moving from room to room in a knowing manner, checking in the cupboards that could double up as hiding places. It's clean in here, given its exterior, not even a speck of dust in sight; I run my finger along the mantelpiece to confirm. There are coasters on the table with the exact same gap in between each one, a faint shadow of a tea ring on only one. The pillows are plump, and the flowers are ripe; with further inspection, I see they are plastic.

Yvonne places her hand on an empty cup by the sink, her eyes avert outside towards the barn. "He's nearby."

The clearly inherited love for tea drew Yvonne to check the lukewarm cup for timings. I frantically look around the kitchen for an easy hiding place to duck in to, in case he returns. My anxiousness is showing through even more, each second, as I scratch the palms of my hand with my nails until they feel raw. The collar on my top is getting tighter and tighter causing an uncontrollable sweat to break out. My heart is beating at such a force, I am afraid it is going to pop out of my chest. The worry that he may kill me wasn't there earlier when I had him in a headlock, one arm twisted around his back, but it's there now, twisting my stomach into all sorts of knots pushing even harder on bladder. Didn't Winnie describe him as super powerful and Yvonne say she knows his skills, that's the reason she wants me to go back. Is there a sick bucket around here. I can feel the peaches making their way back up again.

I don't know what Yvonne is thinking or feeling right now, her expression hasn't changed the whole time here; she's just watching out the window and then there's me. I have gone through every expression on my face, I even smiled.

"The barn doors just opened, get out the house, quick, and down the side."

We get out the house. I have this awful feeling I didn't put the fake flower I took out the vase to look at, back, and I, in fact, put it down on the kitchen table.

"I think I left the flower out; we need to go back."

"We can't go back. He won't notice. We need to hide; stop caring about the flower."

I listen to her but that doesn't mean I trust he won't notice. I've very possibly gave us away.

Chapter Sixteen

We leg it out the door, closing it quickly behind us, careful not to make a loud noise. We hide down the side of the house and duck behind the fence peeking over to check when he is gone.

"What are you doing?" Yvonne asks as I mount the fence, a sudden burst of energy taking hold of my body.

"He's clearly got everyone in the barn, so I'm going there." The confidence I lost, has returned. I jump to the ground on the other side of the fence, escaping the tug on my leg from Yvonne.

"Get back here," she whisper shouts.

"I'm not hiding behind a fence all day. If that's all you want to do, then you may as well go back." I shrug. "Come on Yvonne, climb over."

After a few huffs, eye rolls and attempted threats to throw me in the dungeon if I don't obey, she scrambles over the fence.

"This is ridiculous, we should have waited."

"Waited for what, pigs to fly?" She doesn't get that saying, seeing as she doesn't know what pigs are.

"You do know my father could kill you, without you even knowing if he sees you."

"Well, when you say it like that." I do a one eighty and march back towards the safety fence.

"I don't think so," she pulls me back by the scruff of my top "take this." She hands me the ring with the yellow diamond in, "you'll need it."

"Why?"

"It's powerful and wearing it makes you possess the power."

I struggle to keep up with her long strides.

"I know, Winnie told me, but I don't know how to do any spells, so why will I need it?"

"You don't need to, it knows, seeing as it's the one that has the power and not you. All you have to do is move your arms around and not speak."

'All you have to do is move your arms around and not speak,' that's exactly what Carol said when she saw me talking to the visitors at work. She really doesn't know what a greeter is.

As we trek through the weeds and long grass, I remember what Yvonne said about her dad being a keen gardener, and the tree story; by the looks of it, he's forgotten what a lawn mower is.

I can't count on two hands how many times I have looked behind to check Maxim isn't watching at the kitchen window, or silently lurking behind, ready to strike when right.

Finally, at the barn. The journey felt much longer than Maxim's journey to the house was, he must have gotten a knack for pulling himself through the unkempt garden. I pull the doors open to the barn a small amount, and we creep through the crack, not entirely aware what is on the other side.

I feel sick to my stomach, as I look around the barn. The missing, all slumped on the floor at first, I thought they were dead; the way they are all laid, gave me that thought. Yvonne informed me they are just under a strong curse, after pulling up one of their eyelids and feeling their pulses.

I spot Gertie. I was hoping I got it wrong, she wasn't missing, just fast asleep at home and her alarm is just broken. None of them stir at our arrival or Yvonne's checks. I can't imagine what they went through.

"How do we get them awake?"

"Stand back." Just as she holds out flat palms ready to wake them with a spell, there's movement outside. My heart skips a thousand beats. A lump has appeared in my throat making it hard to breathe. We dive behind a barrel of hay, holding a statue position. I try not to sob too loud as he struts through the door.

Without his hooded cape, I can see his face clear. His looks not faded but aged, his once dark hair greying, his frown lines more dominant and a certain evil twinkle in his eye that isn't there in his portrait at the top of the stairs.

He knows we are here, his head is moving side to side quicker than a butterfly flutters its wings; he noticed the flower, this is all my fault. He counts his prisoners one by one making sure not a single soul escaped his clutches. Maxim steps over the still bodies not caring if he knocks them with his shoe. I grit my teeth when he steps over Gertie, standing on her finger accidently or more possibly on purpose. The red rings make a reappearance around Yvonne's eyes as she watches the man that she loved and respected, show his true colours. Her mouth is slightly curved down and her nose crinkled, fighting back the tears that want to escape. He counts his last victim and makes his way to the door, his ears twitching wanting to catch the slightest noise from us intruders.

His hand hesitates on the door handle, he senses something. My heart is beating more than before and I don't know how that is possible. A drop of sweat drips down my face and the hair on my arms are standing on edge.

We try to manoeuvre around the hay barrels without him knowing, not even allowing a scrape of our foot on the floor. We can no longer see him, our vision is blocked; I'm so scared, scared to the point I am bursting for a wee. I almost sit on Yvonne's knee when I jump back.

I feel a hand rest on my shoulder and it's not Yvonne's.

Chapter Seventeen

Yvonne has reshifted herself, hiding out of sight due to my request; I managed to do a shooing motion with my hand without Maxim noticing and she actually listened. He's hesitated, his hand is still on my shoulder; I've managed to cut the inside of my cheeks from biting them in an attempt to stop my jaw from chattering like a skeleton. He pulls me through the hay barrel, making it rain hay all over us.

"I did wonder when you would be joining us," he rests his forearm over my throat digging it more in with every word, "I see you brought a friend, care to introduce." He stretches his neck upwards to get a better view over my head of the person that is yet to reveal themselves. He's not massively tall, or maybe I am just a lot taller than the average person my age, so he stands around the same height as myself but much more intimidating.

He laughs a harsh evil cackle, it sends shivers down my spine and leaves a drop of saliva on my neck. In a desperate attempt, I try to wipe it away but the movement of my arm causes him to push my head back and cut deeper into my throat with his arm. It's at that moment, Yvonne lifts up from behind the hay, a single tear trickles down her cheek and her eyes are glazed as she dusts the stray hay off her legs, ignoring the tear.

He doesn't recognise his daughter as an adult, without her pigtails and innocent baby face. I widen my eyes at her, hoping she will get the message to run but she doesn't.

"It's me, father."

His mouth drops open and his grip of my neck loosens. I fall to the ground coughing and spluttering from the choking while they have their unpalatable reunion.

"Yvonne, I didn't recognise you."

Her eyes narrow. "I almost didn't recognise you; I think it's that look in your eye." He looks at the ground like a naughty schoolboy being told off by his teacher.

"What are you doing here father? You died, or did you forget that part."

He shakes his head. "I've missed you more than you would care to believe." She looks away. I am sure I heard a single 'ha' escape her mouth. "Believe me when I say it, it's not been easy."

He goes up to her and takes her hands, she hesitates a second before pulling them out of his clasp.

"If you missed me as much as you say you did, you will free everyone and stop this nonsense, return home and explain all of this to me, father to daughter."

He turns his back on her, heavy breathing out of his nose. "I can't."

"You can't or you won't? What happened to you, I don't understand."

"Nothing happened, this is me." He dabs his cheek with his index finger, a mixture of emotions tangled on his face.

"It's not you. You were a happy, family-orientated man, you cared more about everyone else than yourself and not to mention the best gardener there is." She tries and pulls at his heartstrings, hopefully release his good side.

"None of that was me." But he doesn't have a good side and never did. "I didn't have time to garden, it was Heston, and as for caring for everyone but myself, you are very much mistaken. My plan is to take over the land and everyone in it, under my spell they will have to obey me. Sure they obeyed me as king, but Heston was going to ruin that, he was going to out me…" His laughter gives me the same effect as brain freeze. "…Ruin my life, and I wasn't going to let that happen. I needed out and to take him down before he could take me down. After all my dad did want him to be king and not me, it would have put a dampener on my plan if he took the throne.

"Faking your death is easy when you have someone on side. My aide was happy to take orders from her king and spread the news of my death. Course, she wasn't too sure of the plan at first but I spun her a lie about how Heston was after me, it was the only thing that would protect me and my family, blah, blah, blah, and that I would return when Heston was well and truly gone. The poor woman didn't have much life left in her though, died shortly after, so it worked out seamless for me. I spent years working out a plan, I thought I'd get the handiest people out the way first, and then the rest would be easy. You know the only person I ever loved was you, my daughter, but don't think that means I won't go through you to finish what I started if you get in my way." I feel a pain shoot through my arm, as his foot meets my hand at a force, his big boots squishing my fingers beneath them, "And as for the girl, well, it wouldn't hurt me one bit to kill her." The word ‘kill’ rings in my ears and the pain from the stamping forms endless tears in my eyes.

“I won’t let that happen, release the curse that holds them bound, let them move to their own sounds.” Yvonne claps her hands together and releases a rush of power towards the sleeping.

Maxim doesn’t move, he just watches everyone slowly stand, not entirely sure of their surroundings just yet. The heavy nose breathing is back, his lips are pursed tight.

“Why have you done that, Yvonne.”

“Because this is all ridiculous, I know this isn’t you, Dad, I can forgive you.” She is now the one gravitating towards him, grabbing his hands.

“You always were the forgiving type.” He puts his arms around her holding her tight. She copies, resting her head on his shoulder.

“I knew you wouldn’t have it in you to hurt anyone.”

“What did I tell you about forgiving so easily.” The edge of his mouth curves as he grabs the back of her top with a force.

“What!” She tries to pull out of his hug, but he doesn’t let her go.

“Daughter or not, you aren’t coming between my plans.”

I see his arm-twist; I don’t realise what has happened until I see blood dripping on to the floor from a knife that is placed in Maxim’s hand. Even for a split second, I see a hint of shock on his face, but it is soon replaced with nothingness. He holds on to Yvonne, her face growing paler and paler. “I still love you, Yvonne. I didn’t want this to happen but it had to.”

He lets her slip out of his hands. She drops to her knees clutching on to her stomach, her clothes and hands are soaked in blood, her own blood. She tries to speak but her words are staying put. She lays herself down and closes her eyes.

I scramble towards her and put my non-damaged hand on hers, pushing down, creating pressure on her wound.

"It's ok, Yvonne, you'll be ok." I turn towards Maxim, who just stood there, not a sign of regret on his face. "She's your daughter, how could you do that."

"I suggest you all stay here; I won't hesitate to kill the rest of you, don't test me."

Gertie tries to push herself through everyone, her hands in strangling position, but is pulled back by a woman that has similar looking features to herself. Everyone came around properly just as Maxim's hand pulled away from Yvonne's stomach; straight away they caught sight of the bright red liquid sitting on the knife's point.

Gertie's priority has changed from wrapping her hands around Maxim's neck, who is still standing there watching the scene he caused unfold, to seeing how she can help the half-conscious Queen.

I struggle to keep her awake and to stop the blood from seeping onto the floor. Without a second thought for his daughter, I see Maxim at the corner of my eye, wiping away the blood from his knife with a hanky he has pulled from his pocket. He drops the bloodstained hanky on to the floor, then he makes a break for it, not looking back. No one stops him, all eyes are on their Queen. Some are sobbing, feeling helpless, others are comforting and muttering ideas that may help.

"I have an idea, but you need to move your hands."

I follow Gertie's instructions, unaware what her plan could possibly be. Yvonne's eyes close and her pulse grows weak; time is valuable and none of us are wanting to waste a second. I change my strategy from talking a load of nonsense to keep Yvonne awake, to telling her a story my mum used to tell me at night, I always listened till the end. It's about a Queen and how she built a massive castle for herself and lived happily ever after. It has that twist on a story tale that I like.

Gertie blows into her own hand catching a gold air and enclosing it in. The woman that pulled Gertie back, kneels by her side.

"Are you sure, Granny?"

Gertie turns to face her granddaughter, "I'm old, Tamsin, she needs it more than me, and less of the Granny. I told you to call me G." She lets out a half-hearted laugh.

Tamsin gives her grandma a pat on the shoulder and a sweet smile then stands up and moves away, leaving Gertie to it.

"What are you doing, Gertie?" I ask, unsure if I want to know the answer.

"No time to explain but I promise I will let you know."

She releases the gold air on to Yvonne's body and it clings to her like a shield. I watch on as the magic slowly pulls the colour back in to her skin. There is no more blood making its way out of her now-healed wound. There's only the bloodstain and the hole on her top that shows signs that something happened. We wait, everyone leaning in for closer inspection, waiting for that first pulse of the chest.

Yvonne's eyes fly open and her breathing starts again, heavy but there. Gertie looks at me and smiles, but her eyes are glazed with tears; I get this weird feeling that what she did wasn't good for herself. Yvonne props herself up on her elbows, looking down at her ex-wound.

"Where's Dad?" she says, looking around the room at the happy crowd. How can she still call him Dad after that, I don't know. He's more an enemy.

"He ran off." I stand up, an ache in my knees from the cold hard floor, "And now that you are okay, I'm going to go find him."

"Not on your own, you're not." Gertie rises but her steps are unsteady. "You aren't going off on your own again, we are coming."

"No, you aren't. I was brought here to save you all and I am not risking a single one of your deaths." I go over to Gertie and wrap my arms around her. "If I don't come back it was a pleasure being your sidekick, Gertie."

"We all know I am your sidekick." I shake my head in disagreement, "I just followed you."

The door is locked but it's no struggle to get out. Yvonne uses the little energy she has gained back, to give one swish of her finger that unlocks the door. I give her the adult nod of the head. This is the time when I am needed, really needed.

Chapter Eighteen

The grounds are clear; well, the grounds around the house are clear, having an allotted time to search an area as best as possible is difficult. I barge my way through the door to Maxim's house, not caring about the hole in the wall the door handle caused, due to the force.

"Come on, Maxim, you stabbed your own daughter, can't you come up against a fifteen-year-old with no powers and a possible broken hand?" I take a quick peek around the living room door and then the kitchen, there's stuff all over the floor in both room. He must have taken his stress out on the furniture.

I hear a noise upstairs. The temptation to go up boils inside me, but there is something telling me to wait. I put my foot on the first step, a trembling hand on the railing, I am not sure if I am scared or angry, possibly both. The squeak the floorboards on the first step made, seem to have triggered him to show himself.

"If you get out of my way and leave now, I'll let you live." He stands rigid on the top step his fists clenched.

"And what about everyone else, are they allowed to live." I create a barrier with my arms knowing full well he can just push past me or just use some magic.

"I'm not in a bargaining mood it's you or no one. I will send you back to your land and you can go back to whatever sad life you lead."

"Who died and made you king?" his eyebrows raise slightly at my reply. "Yvonne didn't die and she's not going to, so I'm not moving."

He hesitates, rubbing his lips together and gulping hard.

"Don't tempt me to kill you and don't think I am stupid either, I know you have the diamond." His eyes flicker towards my unbroken hand that possesses the ring. "You have guts, I'll give you that, coming up against me with power you have no idea how to use or whether it will adjust to you." The stomach twisting feeling has returned.

"You know what, I'll do you a deal. Join me, you can keep the diamond. I'll teach you the ways and Gertie and her family can live but that's as far as I'll go. It's not like Gertie has much life left anyway. She'll soon be joining the rest of her family in the forest. I did want her originally to drain her of the rest of her life so I can live for longer; hers will be easier to take with her being old, her family's would be much harder but not impossible; with you by my side., my legacy will live on through you, so I won't need them."

"You know what, I don't think I am in a bargaining mood as well. If you think for a second I believe you will let them go and I will actually join you, then you are as stupid as you look."

He starts making his way down the stairs; I stand there holding my ground.

"Very well, death might not be as painful as you think. I'll make it quick." He cracks his knuckles and neck preparing himself so he can make me meet my doom.

I grab a vase off a table and throw it at him. It narrowly misses and shatters against the wall behind him. I make a run for it, ducking his spells that are skimming my head, singeing the end of my hair. I make it out the house and into the open land, unscathed, but I don't stop running; he's following fast. I try to change directions, throw him off course, but he's not falling for it, his spells are still coming my way quicker than before.

My head feels heavy and I am roasting, it's like I am running but not actually going anywhere. I haven't breathed in a few minutes; I think I have forgotten how to breathe. I am silently begging for someone to come to my rescue.

My foot gives way due to my poor-quality shoes, and no air. I struggle to get back up with the only hand that has strength. The spells have stopped, and I don't know what that means. Has he stopped running? Has he seen some sense? Will he be letting me go? I doubt it, I bet he is near and is wanting me to see my death, up close, look into my eyes as he takes my life.

I can hear his loud stomps now; they sound like a drum beating in my ears. He grabs my hair, yanking me upwards like a rag doll, I can feel strands leaving my head. It's like I have serious carpet burn.

"Please, let me go," I plead, gritting my teeth hard through the pain.

He holds a finger to my cheek. His nail is piercing my skin. "Did your parents ever tell you, it's rude to throw things?"

The pain from my fear is crippling. I can only hear the beat of my heart. I stand in his grasp whimpering and snivelling trying to plan a way out in my mind that's so fogged, I can barely remember my name.

I take a plunge and kick him as hard as possible in the ankle. I pull myself out of his grasp as he bends down to hold his ankle, leaving him with a clump of my hair in between his fingers. I sense a trickle of blood gliding down my cheek, caused by a harsh scratch from his nail.

He doesn't look so happy about the kicking. "It's a shame you can't say a goodbye to your parents," his words make me stop running and come to a surprising halt, to both of us.

"Why would I need to say goodbye?" I don't feel like myself.

I throw my hands back, ignoring the desperate cry for attention from my hand and without a second thought, I launch them forward. My swing is effortless, just like waving.

The power that possesses me, moves through my veins; my whole body feels like it's on fire. I have been taken over and the next moves won't be my own, instead they will be the concealed power of Oaky. The agony in my hand is gone, as my fingers are tingling, like when you have been laid on your arm when you're asleep. A burst of purple, rockets out my hands while everything else moves in slow motion. There's no time for Maxim to move, the light hits him square in the chest. I see the hope of defeating me leave his eyes and replaced with shock and panic. For a moment, I feel sympathy, mainly for Yvonne losing her dad once again, even though he is filled with pure evil. I don't know what I have used on him, it's not looking clever. He drops to his knees, his face dripping, literally dripping; I think I have melted him.

At this point, Yvonne, Gertie, and everyone else are running from the barn. Yvonne spots her dad, but she doesn't try to stop what is happening; she watches the man that betrayed her melt. Maxim tries to hold out his hand to Yvonne, but it’s too late, his arm dissolves leaving nothing but a puddle.

Chapter Nineteen

No one says anything, not even Gertie and she has something to say about everything. I can see gritted teeth and finger twiddling, no one quite sure what to say. Everyone's eyes are looking elsewhere, except Yvonne; the puddle that was once Maxim, even I can't look at him. We must be well into the night now, there's no ombre sunset, but midnight blue skies.

"I don't know what I did, Yvonne, he was going to kill me. I just let the diamond do it," the words came out in a whisper.

"It's fine," she bites her bottom lip and looks up, "You had to. He definitely would have killed you, I have no doubt about that, it's just a shock."

"What did I do, what happened to him?"

"It's a spell to remove all the evil from someone's bones; seeing as he is all evil, he melted completely. No one has ever had that much evil in them for it to actually melt them. I saw the purple light, so I knew what was happening."

"I'm sorry."

"Why?"

"I killed him."

"No you didn't, he did this to himself."

I just about conjure a smile in return to hers.

Gertie hooks my arm and leads me away. We all exit through the tree and back to reality. We left Maxim to fade into the ground and become a part of the soil, what else was there to do? There's mixed emotions in the air. Those that haven't seen their families and friends in a while are beyond excited to see them again, but also must explain Maxim's return and defeat, which means a million and two questions. I can hear them telling each other their replies. Yvonne is pretending she isn't listening but her ears must be burning. Her head tilts slightly in the direction of those mentioning her name or Maxim's in low whispers.

We ignore the gawping gossipers that have congregated outside their houses, hair in rollers and their nightgowns on. Eyes are stuck on the Queen's blood stained top, coming up with their own scenarios but not daring to ask questions.

One by one, the group disband, back to their homes, making their appreciation clear, and thanking us endlessly. Pointis looks over the moon at his neighbour's return, pulling her in for a long embrace, his cheeks are rather rosy. I saw him lift her hair up and give it a sniff without her realising, which is strange but maybe that's how he shows his affection, still strange. He gave me a thumbs-up along with the widest smile I think he could possibly muster. Gertie hugs all her family, while Yvonne and I wait at a distance to give them their private space.

"Have you seen our Queen, drenched in blood? Look, there's a slit in her top as well."

"You don't think she got stabbed, that new girl's hands are stained as well. I'll wait half hour and drop by Tiger Lily's house; her son went missing, she will definitely know what happened."

“I will join you; I’ll throw a robe on and grab one of my home-made cakes.” They scurry off back into their houses. I can only imagine she has a cupboard full of cakes on standby, just in case she needs to hurry around to someone’s house to stick her nose in where it’s not wanted. Can’t really blame them though. Gertie returns and we set off walking again, in tune to the talkers.

As we approach the gates, the guards see us and stand up so fast off their stools, they clap heads. I felt the pain so much that I actually rubbed my forehead.

“Queen. What happened, you’re bleeding?”

“I’m not. Well, not anymore.” She looks down at the no longer pristine white top, running her finger down the slit.

The Guards attempt to rush to her aid, but she bats them off. “I’m fine, really, thanks to those two.” Gertie can’t help but be smug in front of the guards and so she should be. “In the morning, I would like to do a speech to the land. 9 am will be fine. Could you arrange that for me?”

“Of course.”

“Thank you, now I think it’s time for bed. Gertie if you would like, we have a spare bedroom made up. You must be exhausted, and I would really appreciate it if you would accompany me in my speech tomorrow, if you please.”

“I’d be honoured to, Yvonne.” Gertie gives me an elbow in the ribs while bobbing her eyebrows up and down. It’s either because she’s staying at the house on the Queen’s request or because she’s on a first name basis with the Queen and didn’t get told off.

Do I want to talk about what happened, I’m not sure. Technically, I killed a man with a power beyond me and that will live with me forever. I can still feel the tingle in my fingers and feel the warmth from the magic hitting my face. That moment will be forever tattooed on my mind. It has wiped out the only scary thing I ever experienced before this day, from my brain, which has stuck like glue for some time now; I was playing with a wooden slingshot in the back garden when I was younger, and I was really good at getting stuff to go far, unfortunately, my talent let me down when I decided to sling a rock and it hit my neighbour's window and completely shattered it. Luckily, behind our gardens is open land, so I lied, and said it was some kids. My parents or Richard never found out and I hid my slingshot, never to be used again; it doesn't feel so bad now.

"I know what you are thinking." Gertie is staring at me as we make our way up to our bedrooms. My mind is racing ahead, but my legs are moving at normal speed. Seeing as she doesn't know about the slingshot story, I don't think she's talking about that.

"Am I a murderer?" my words slip out before I can catch them.

"No, you are a life saver, if anything. Who knows what he would have done if any of us stepped out of line."

We stop in front of the portrait of Maxim. I look up at him, so much more different than the first time I saw this picture. "He said he would let me, you and your family go free. I said no."

I don't remove my eyes from his face, his still image seems to be melting as well, over and over again.

"I wouldn't have been very happy with you if you had said yes." Gertie is looking at Maxim also, her eyes are daggers.

"What happened to you all, when you were taken?"

“I refused the guards help back to my house, course my memory has gaps in it, thanks to the wine, but I just remember stumbling home and next second a hand slaps on to my mouth. I struggled but was unable to get free. My eyes started to feel heavy, like I hadn’t slept for a long time, then I woke up as I was being pushed through the barn doors. I saw my family slumped on the floor, I tried to get to them and then nothing; the next thing I know, I’m waking once more to you lot standing in front of me. I thought I was dreaming at first, couldn’t believe my eyes when I saw Maxim stood there, alive and well.”

“I felt the exact same when I tackled him to the floor earlier on. Gertie, what did you do back there, how did you save Yvonne?”

Her eyes close while she gathers her words.

“Sometimes you have to do things that may not benefit yourself, to save others. I lived a long and happy life. I want that for Yvonne.”

“Are you going to die?” I let a tear escape and slide down my cut cheek. Gertie’s eyes concentrate on the tear and back to my eyes.

“I will never really die; I don’t like that word; no one ever really dies, they always live on,” she leaves me on that note and goes off to her room. I don’t attempt to carry on the questions. I have a feeling she’s not ready for that.

Chapter Twenty

I haven't slept a wink. I just laid in bed all night, the covers pulled tightly over my neck; I don't even think I blinked. My eyes are aching. It was really hot the whole time, but the covers were my shield and I couldn't remove it.

The time is 7:13 am. I have counted every single flower on the ugly wallpaper across from my bed, four hundred and twenty-three give or take, a few when my mind fell in to thought.

I kept wondering if I should tell my parents what has happened. Of course, they will want to know where I have been, but do I tell them the truth or a lie. I can't even think of what lie I would use (and they call me the liar) but they wouldn't even believe the truth if I told it them, I am struggling to believe what is happening and I am here. I am already prepared to be grounded for eternity. I have missed them though, so much more than I ever thought I would. I do know how they feel now when they ask me so many questions and don't get the reply they want; my whole time here I have asked loads of questions and only received half-hearted answers; to say it winds me up is an understatement.

I can hear lots of speaking outside the window. I remove my shield, flinching at the teeth-gritting pain that gushed through my hand and like a kid following a tray of freshly baked cookies leaving the oven, I stalk the voices. There's a crowd already. Lots of pushes trying to get to the front, desperate faces pulling their kids through small gaps, so they aren't stuck at the back, carrying their children on their shoulders. I catch a child's eye who pulls at her dad's top and points in my direction. I've never ducked so fast in my life; my broken hand didn't thank me.

I quickly get changed and go downstairs. I hear talking in the living room and as a professional eavesdropper, experience gained from listening in on my parents conversations about my behaviour, I'm going to put my ear against the door. I know they will go all hush hush if I go through the door, seeing as my invite to the conversation didn't make it.

I can hear Yvonne's voice, "When do you think it will happen?"

Now Gertie's, "I don't know. I feel weaker by the hour. I suppose by the end of the day I should make my way to the forest."

"Are you going to tell Adalyn? I know you have grown close, but she will be leaving, anyway?"

"She knows something has happened; she's a clever one. Mrs Read made the right decision." I blush.

"Yes, she did. I couldn't have taken my father down, no matter how." There's hesitation. "Evil he was. I knew if I gave the diamond to Adalyn, she would have it, if need be. She's strong, the diamond wouldn't have listened to her cry for help if she wasn't."

"Stronger than any of us here; you can be just as powerful without power"

"Agreed."

"Hi, Adalyn." Winnie appears behind me. Does everyone round here creep around, my heart has just fell out. "What's happened, are you spying?"

"Erm, what, no, I am admiring the door, apparently oak speaks to you. I am just listening to it."

The one eyebrow up tells me she didn't buy it. "It's not oak."

"Did I say oak?" I laugh rather loud and exaggerated. "I meant, erm..."

The door opens and I am saved, the only wood I know is oak, but I know for sure it doesn't talk to you.

"Adalyn, Winnie, I thought I heard you. Is everything ok?"

"It's fine. The crowd outside is rather loud and big."

"Ah, yes, the crowd. What time we on?" She doesn't wait for anyone to answer. "I best get prepared."

"Me too," I put my hand on Gertie's forehead stopping her from going any further.

"Gertie, I want answers."

"For what?"

"For the test I have on the first day back home schooling, the one my teacher told me to revise for."

"I don't think I can help you with that one." She whips a biscuit out her pocket and it goes in her mouth whole.

"You know what I am talking about; I want answers, biscuit or no biscuit in your mouth."

"Fine," she's just spat a load of sloppy biscuit onto my face.

"Actually, no biscuit," I say this while wiping away her spit from my eye, ewww.

“Sorry,” she showered me and Winnie this time.

“Eat your biscuit and then we will speak.”

We sit down opposite each other in the living area like I am interviewing her, she takes the final swallow and that is my queue to speak.

“Why are you going to the forest later? Maxim said something about you joining your family in the forest, but I didn’t think anything of it, until I heard you speaking to Yvonne.”

“Were you snooping?”

“That’s not the point. Please, tell me the truth. I can’t leave without knowing.”

“My family don’t die; we are seeds, we grow, and we grow until we are the perfect tree and when our time comes that’s what we will be. I gave my final bit of life to Yvonne so now my time has come, well actually, my time was coming fast any way, I had months, if that. Twiddlestone forest is the forest of my family. Generations of my family have been born, raised and then went on to their next lives. It’s how it is, there’s no way to stop it and I wouldn’t if I could. We live a longer life than anyone here, it’s not as though I am young, although my good looks have not faded. I will grow my branches and move on to my next adventure, reunited with my past family, together forever. You mentioned the trees greeted you when you arrived, they are a friendly bunch. None of them have the humour I do though. I’d like to tickle people on the back and make them wonder who it was, that’s if we get any more visitors. I’ll still be me, just as a tree.”

I don’t know if I should cry or not, after all she seems happy about it. I pull Gertie into the biggest hug I can muster.

"I haven't known you for a long time, Gertie, but you made me feel at home even though mine is so far away. Knowing you would be around living your life back with your family made it that bit more easy, leaving."

"I will be with my family and living my life, just the second part of it. Don't worry about me."

"I never worry about you; I don't have anything to worry about."

The situation is bittersweet; everything about this whole situation being here is bittersweet. I feel like I am in a bag of emotions which is being shook constantly and I want to get out and just go home, go to bed and dread normal stuff like school and work.

"Sorry to intrude. Would any one like any breakfast and tea?"

"What a silly question, Winnie. Of course I want breakfast; put a plate of biscuits on the side as well, please."

"But Gertie your pocket is full of them." Gertie just gave me the worst look ever.

"You just crushed them with your hug, they are just mere crumbs."

We sat and waited for Winnie to come back and as for Gertie's crushed biscuits, they are not so crushed. I can see her sneaking ones out of her pocket and putting them in her mouth thinking I can't see; it is funny though, asking her question while she has the biscuit in her mouth and seeing how she deals with it.

Winnie returns with a tray each, she made goop, not appetising, and that's just the scent. Why's it green?

"What is this?"

"It's my homemade porridge."

"Oh," Winnie looks happy about it and I'd feel bad if I didn't at least give it a try.

I scoop some up and it instantly makes me want to puke looking at it close up. Winnie is standing, smiling at me waiting for me to eat it. Gertie seems to be enjoying it surely, it's not that bad then. It's bad, it's really bad! My jaw won't stop quivering; the texture is so slimy, it's how I imagine eating a snail, without the shell, would be.

"Enjoying it?"

"Um." I give thumbs up because I daren't swallow it.

"It's the first time I have made it. I added some special ingredients in."

All I can do is nod and try and stop it from sliding down my throat. She leaves finally, and I spit it back into the bowl straight away.

"It's not nice, is it?" Gertie throws her spoon down and pushes the bowl along the table.

"But you nearly ate it all."

"I've been given some horrible stuff in my time. I have a strong stomach."

"Where shall I dispose of it?"

"In the plant, by time she realises, we'll both be gone any way." I got a shiver in my spine when she said, 'we'll both be gone.

The clock reads 8:50, so I pour my bowl of slush in the plant and apologise to the plant while doing so and we prepare our self for the speech.

Chapter Twenty-One

I lurk in the background while Yvonne and Gertie stand centre, in front of the gates. Gertie ushers me to go forward but I politely decline. I am not an all-eyes-on me kind of person; I am a background role, surprisingly.

The crowd goes silent as Yvonne clears her throat.

"Good morning, thank you all for coming, I presume you have all heard stories and rumours, some possibly true but most false. So, I thought I should put those to rest. So, I won't waste any more time. My father returned, he never died." She ignores the gasps. "He was the reason for the disappearances and every bad word about Heston was a lie, no murder or attempted murder took place and what Heston said about the throne being his, it was true. Settle, everyone, settle."

"He is not evil, Maxim is," she coughs, "was. Maxim is no longer around and never will be again," she choked on those words. "He wanted to create a land controlled by him, make you all his puppets, but he lost the battle thankfully. I can only apologise for the distress and pain he caused, both to those he took and their families and friends. We will move on and grow stronger. I'd like to publicly thank Gertie; without her, I wouldn't be alive and, Adalyn, our guest of honour, for risking her life for a land that isn't her own. Thank you both, once again." She leaves the crowd wanting more and exits the grounds. By Gertie's expression and lack of movement, she was expecting more speech as well.

Yvonne strides past me, but doesn't acknowledge my existence. I waved and smiled at her but had to turn it in to an arm stretch. I wait and watch the crowd disband slowly, some lingerers wait at the gates, I presume, hoping for the Queen's encore, like at a concert when the act goes off stage, so everyone starts to leave, then the lights go down and they appear on stage again and belt out some more songs. I've never been to a concert, but I have watched live performances on the TV and they all do it. Somehow, I don't think Yvonne is going to do an encore. When Queen Elizabeth does her yearly Christmas speech, I can only presume she doesn't go and come back again. Then again, I have never paid much attention. I am always in a Christmas dinner coma by that time.

I saw the front page of a newspaper the other day, on one of the stands outside a shop, it read, 'The Queen—does she have a voice?' I bet that's one of the reasons most of the people got here so early, the Queen's first speech. It must be hard for her, all that has happened through her life, being made Queen so young, and being on her own for so long, then this happens.

"Adalyn, can I have a chat?" It seems Yvonne has caught the creeping bug. I never used to be a chatting person but that's all I do nowadays. The last lingerers leave, having realised Yvonne isn't returning.

Yvonne doesn't wait for me to reply and goes away to the empty living room, no Gertie in sight. I zoned out, focusing on the people at the gates and when I zoned back in, she was gone.

"Tea?"

"No, thanks." She drinks more tea than my dad and that's saying something.

"I'm sorry, I didn't believe you about my dad's return at first."

"I don't blame you. I'd be the same if it was me," I'd be more surprised my dad could come up with a plan like that. When he gets angry at a wooden table he can't put up, he blames it on the table for him hitting his thumb with a hammer.

"I want you to know that it isn't your fault, what happened. The ring doesn't take directions from you, not really, it senses scenarios and realises when you are asking for help. It uses the best spell for the situation. Oaky was clever, he knew what he was doing."

"I'd like to have met Oaky, he sounds terrific."

"Me too," her voice is warm, for the first time since I've been here, possibly while she's been Queen. She sounds relaxed, that weight that took up home on her shoulders has finally been lifted. "I can't unlove my father just like that. It sounds crazy. He stabbed me and left me to die, I spent so many years missing and loving him." She puts her hand where her stab wound once was. "It's not that easy to say goodbye," her stone face has cracked; she is showing her innocence and insecurities. "My mother died of a broken heart from losing him, she cared so dearly about him and couldn't imagine living without him. I'd hear her crying every night, she never slept." Yvonne is staring at the corner of the room clearly remembering her past so vividly in her mind. "I'd walk out my room most days and she'd just be staring at his portrait, her eyes so swelled, her skin pale and her heart unable to mend. I didn't recognise her; I lost her the day I thought I lost my dad and he didn't even care about her after all. I can't wrap my head around that."

I throw caution to the wind. "You need people around you. Open up, there's people out there that will help get you through it, that's what you need; not just Winnie, to serve you food but friends. You can sit there and keep yourself to yourself, sit on your emotions and pretend they aren't there, or you can go out there and seek help. Having the label of Queen means nothing; we all need someone, sometimes, and that's okay. Asking for help doesn't mean you aren't strong, it just means you need reminding of how strong you actually are." I should listen to my own words once in a while.

"You're right, you are. I close myself off; I tried to tell myself I didn't need anyone else."

"You could also find Heston, gather some troops. Surely, he is somewhere, and he is your family."

"I completely forgot, I should. He has been treated awful; I miss him. We were close once upon a time, it's a shame Maxim ruined that out of spite."

"I have a question. How come Maxim was never found, if the place he was hiding was known?"

"The royals were so fascinating when the land was first made, there needed to be a place we could be free, and Trees make the best passageways, so no one knew that tree is an entrance to another part except the royals. I never thought to go look. I didn't want to face the memories, the happy ones. I just pretended it didn't exist; it was easier that way. I did wonder if Heston was there, but I just ignored it."

Now, I am not one to think what if, but there's a first for everything. What if Yvonne went to the hidden place and found her dad; would he still be alive now? Would I have even been brought here?

"I presume you want to know how you will be getting home."

"It is something I have on my mind." She doesn't need to know about my what ifs.

"Here's a door that will take you back. I don't know how time works in your land unfortunately. Would you like to leave now?"

"I'd actually like to say goodbyes first, if that's ok?"

"Certainly."

"Do you know where Gertie is?"

"I'd head to Twiddlestone forest, if I was you." I know what that means, and it hurts.

"How do I get there?"

"Follow me."

I pass Winnie on the way out and bid farewell, she said, "See you soon". I just smiled.

The streets are filled with happy people, even the sun looks extra perky, with the clouds fluffier than ever. All shops are back open, they all look divine as we pass. A young girl hands myself, and Yvonne, a lovely orange flower and runs off, proud of herself.

Yvonne greets everyone as she passes. You could have poked them with a stick and they would have fell down, they are all that shocked at her upbeat attitude. To say I am always called negative Nancy by my parents, I can sure spread some positivity around; they should call me positive Penelope.

I will miss these streets; they aren't lined with rubbish and it's bright and welcoming, clothes shops are lacking but I can get past that. Okay, there are a lot of gossipers but they have nothing on the seeing eye that lives down the road from me, if you so much as trip in front of her, she will spread it far and wide, but add her own little spin on it, like you had a bottle of alcohol in your hand and was drunk, but in fact you're just clumsy.

We arrive at an ugly shed. A man with horns, rather small, angry look on his face and a fishy smell hanging around him, sat messing with some sticks. He looks like a slippery character.

"Hello, Elgo, we would like to go to Twiddlestone, if you please."

"Of course, mam."

I don't think there is any need for him to look me up and down when he is the one sporting extremely hairy legs and some food stained short, not to mention his fish scent has attached itself to my nostrils.

Yvonne goes in the shed first, then me, and followed by grumpy legs.

"I know about you," huh, what does he know about me, "trouble." Has he been speaking with Carol?

"You are very much mistaken."

Yvonne goes through the back of the cramped needy shed and disappears. Weird.

"Go then, silly child, do you think I have all day."

"Excuse me, but I am far from silly and yes, I do think you have all day."

I go through the back of the shed before he can slate me some more and to escape the odour, it's bad. A lot of things smell here and that is something I will not miss.

"Ignore him, he doesn't like people but what he lacks in smiles and politeness, he makes up for in knowledge, very clever."

"Can I take him back with me and show my parent what the real definition of moody is."

She laughs, but it is to be kind, she doesn't get it.

We are in the forest made up of Gertie's family, which sounds hella strange and sad. They are waving and now I know they are actually waving, and it's not just how the branches move. I don't know what to do with myself. It's still captivating.

I spy Gertie and her family, sitting in a little circle on the floor in an empty spot, which I am guessing is now Gertie's place. She sees us, but doesn't stand.

"Hello you two, I've been waiting for you. Join us."

We sit down next to her family members, Yvonne very delicately so. She does have an expensive looking dress on which doesn't look like it should be sat on the floor, she doesn't look like she should sit on the floor as well.

"Goodbyes are hard and pointless because I am not really going anywhere. I'm just going to chill as a tree for a while."

"Like you do," I joke.

"Yep, like you do. I'm old," she said the old part directly to me, she doesn't forget easily, does she? "You'll get bored of me soon, any way, you can come talk to me whenever you want and I won't talk your face off in return or take all your biscuits. I don't know why you are all crying; be happy, we are free now. Adalyn, it has been a pleasure to meet you, you make sure you put that Carol in her place and show her who's boss, release your sass. You're a clever girl, no one here will forget you soon. I wasn't going to tell you about the whole tree issue. I wanted you to sit there in your land and try and imagine how many packets of biscuits I've got through, but I knew you weren't going to leave until I told you the truth. It's why we got on so well." She takes my hand and holds it tight in her warm hands warming my heart as well. "I have enough life in myself to fix that broken hand of yours." She takes my broken hand and at first her clutch made the pain worse, but before I can even wince the pain is gone.

"Yvonne, you don't know how adored you are; your mum will be so proud. You made me one happy person being on a first name basis with a royal, first one out of the lot of us. My family, well, I said it all before these two got here. Now, I don't want you lot sticking around. It will be awkward turning into a tree around you all. I love you all, no goodbyes."

One last hug and one wet shoulder, Gertie now has, the number of tears that have dropped, you could fill a pool. I must look like a wet potato; my eyes are for sure swollen and my face aches.

We hold hands as we drift away from Gertie. I've never lost anyone before and I don't want to ever again, please, it hurts too much. It wouldn't have been so painful if I was just leaving them behind there may have been a chance we would reunite one day but it's not going to happen. I'll never see those cheeks, stuffed full of biscuits again.

We stay in Twiddlestone but away from the forest, I don't like the fact that she's on her own. In a blink of an eye there's a brand-new tree standing tall, leaves greener than all the rest and the branches waving crazily, as though she is saying she's okay and that makes me okay. The tears stop; there's not a single sob coming from anyone.

"Do you want to leave now, Adalyn?"

My nod is my unspoken response.

Chapter Twenty-Two

So, the door I go through was in Yvonne's pocket. She put it on the floor, did a swish with her finger and now there's a larger door sitting on the floor, where the small one once was. She also did another swish and a bunch of balloons appear, hovering by the closed door.

So, my time has come to leave the land that, yes, I nearly died in, but it let me see the breath-taking and the magic that does exists! I got introduced to unicorns, which I will never, ever, ever, get over; it's a shame I can't tell anyone. The best part was getting to meet my best friend. Course there is a massive age gap, but she definitely didn't act it. I felt like the adult the majority of the time. I never thought I would be the grown-up one.

I bid my farewells to those around and the tree that stands the tallest.

"Keep the ring. You never know when you will need it," Yvonne places the ring in my hand and closes it.

"Thank you for being so welcoming. You have one hell of a land, you should be proud; it will take a lot to forget it any time soon, bye."

I let Gertie's wave be the last thing I see.

The group of smiling faces disappear behind me. I close my eyes and allow the portal to take me home. I have an urge to start singing. I keep my eyes closed as I move at a speedy pace through who knows what. I am being too much of a coward to open my eyes. It feels like I am on a roller-coaster but not strapped in just moving round the bends, defying gravity. I am travel sick times a million right now; what would happen if I be sick. Will it stay or travel with me. This is something I am not keen to find out but also can't help thinking about. I may find it out very soon though.

I give in to the temptation and open my eye very small to take a little peek and I think I may be inside a swirling rainbow, very weird indeed. My eyes are staying closed for the rest of the ride. I am dropping faster, like when I fell through the sky, I didn't like it then, and I don't like it now.

I can see my garden. The voices of my parents' chattering away in the kitchen. I have returned to my natural habitat. The familiar surrounding triggers feelings. I am sitting on the same patch of grass I was, when I left; the book laid in front of me, wordless once more. If I wasn't in different clothes (which I am not happy about because the clothes I went in were my favourite and I have left them behind, it's not like they can mail them to me), it would be like I never left.

"Adalyn, come and help a sec," my dad's words confuse me which isn't new, but they confuse me as in why is he okay with my sudden return and why is he wearing the same outfit he was when I left.

I make my way hesitantly to the kitchen. Am I going to get shouted at? I am being led into false pretences.

"Mum, Dad."

"What?" Oh, how I missed them, I really did.

"Adalyn have you changed your clothes; we aren't at a fashion show. I have told you to stop wearing everything in one day."

I don't know what is happening.

"What day is it?"

"The same day it was when you went outside and hid behind the bush."

"28th of August?"

"Yes. What is this, Adalyn? You trying to get out of helping? This isn't cute, you are helping whether you want to or not."

"I've actually got to be somewhere. I missed you both so much."

"You have just been outside, why do you miss us; am I missing something?" She turns to Dad. "Jerry have you told her to do this because if you have, then it's not funny."

"Why would I tell her to act weird. She can do that all on her own."

"I've got to go."

"Wait, where are you going? Why do you have a cut on your cheek?"

I have missed those twenty questions. I run out the house, down the path, and into the streets, leaving the calls from my parents behind. The streets don't feel the same anymore. I am noticing grass and all the wonderful parts not just the rubble and the distasteful. The sun is hiding behind a cloud, so I have no choice but to let the cold lift the hairs on my arms. It feels quite pleasing, though it's been rather hot in Tandalet, so I appreciate the chill.

I am running to the bookshop to visit an acquaintance. I have tripped numerous times and twisted my ankle on more than one occasion, so when I say I am running, it is more a limp run. I'd say seventy-thirty in favour of the limp.

Mrs Read sat on a stool, not actually doing a thing. To say it is busy today around the shops, there's not a single customer in here.

I stop to gather my breath and let the stitch die down before I conjure a sentence of some sense; why do I run when it hurts?

"I've just come from Tandalet."

She just nods.

"And it was Maxim."

She nods again.

"Heston isn't bad and Gertie's a tree," My words are coming out more of a huff due to me struggling to catch my breath. I don't know how she is managing to hear me.

"How was your adventure?"

Her fashion sense hasn't improved, not that I expected it to, but I saw worse in Tandalet. That's including my nightgown.

"I turned Maxim into a puddle."

"So you saved the day."

"I guess. Why did you give me the book?" I'm basically asking, 'Why did you give me all that stress and pressure, but also so much happiness and memories.'

"Because I knew you would save the day."

"I didn't have as much belief in myself as you did."

"Yes, belief is a big thing and that I did have in you. You wouldn't have gotten through the book if you didn't believe it is something more than just an empty book. Tandalet wouldn't have been created if Oaky didn't believe that he possessed a power, something a bit extra than the average person should have somewhere, we could be free, no more hiding. If I didn't believe the person I loved, loved me enough back, for me to leave Tandalet and create a new life here, then I wouldn't have spent the most unforgettable years with someone so special. If you believe in something, then you succeed. I succeeded in life."

I didn't realise how much impact one word could do.

"Do you miss Tandalet?"

"Every day, but I wouldn't go back. I changed my story so that's it. It ended here with my family."

I have a desire to ask multiple questions, but for once the desire to dig further into someone's life doesn't interest me and in fact mystery is more interesting this time.

"Keep the book; it's time I pass on the baton to someone worthy. But keep an eye on it because pages don't stay blank forever."

Chapter Twenty-Three

I ponder down the park path, noting the differences between here and Tandalet in the notebook called my mind. The plants seem to flop here. I may come and secretly garden this park back to life.

I sit down on the same bench I seem to always gravitate to and risk closing my eyes. I may open them to a child using my face as a colouring book or a weird fly thing hovering around my head.

I didn't know air could feel so different in one place to another. In Tandalet, the air smelt so scented and fresh (well, most places) but here it smells like a bin, given I am sitting next to one. I just realised I didn't see any bins in Tandalet at all, but there was no rubbish on the floor anywhere, strange. This has been one of the longest days of my life and it's still only morning.

"Hello again," the voice sounds familiar, "did you figure out the book."

It's the old man I met before; he's dressed very dapper wearing a white shirt with a brown check blazer and not to forget the matching hat.

"Hi, I did. It was much more than a book."

"I knew you would figure it out, things that don't make sense always make sense in the end."

"Did you finish your jigsaw?"

"I did, one of the pieces got trapped in the box. I didn't know though, thought it was gone forever, only found it today. I saw it as a sign, today is going to be my day, thought I'd treat myself to a trip down to my favourite bench. It seems we both accomplished something, doesn't it."

"It seems we did."

We both go silent and watch the river travel.

"I never asked your name, how rude of me. I'm Adalyn."

We shake hands his grip is firm.

"Tolstem, Heston Tolstem."

The End